DISCARD

THE PRICE OF LOVE

THE PRICE OF LOVE

Helen McCabe

CHIVERS
THORNDIKE

This Large Print book is published by BBC Audiobooks Ltd, Bath, England and by Thorndike Press®, Waterville, Maine, USA.

Published in 2005 in the U.K. by arrangement with the author.

Published in 2005 in the U.S. by arrangement with Helen McCabe.

U.K. Hardcover ISBN 1–4056–3373–5 (Chivers Large Print)
U.S. Softcover ISBN 0–7862–7632–0 (British Favorites)

The text of this Large Print edition is unabridged.
Other aspects of the book may vary from the original edition.

Set in 16 pt. New Times Roman.

Printed in Great Britain on acid-free paper.

British Library Cataloguing in Publication Data available

Library of Congress Cataloging-in-Publication Data

McCabe, Helen.
    The price of love / by Helen McCabe.
        p.   cm.
    "Thorndike Press large print British favorites."—T.p. verso.
    ISBN 0–7862–7632–0 (lg. print : sc : alk. paper)
    1. Businesswomen—Fiction. 2. Large type books. I. Title.
    PR6113.C35P75 2005
    823'.92—dc22   2005004937

CHAPTER ONE

'Day-dreaming, dear? That's not like you!' Lady Melling said, her eyes twinkling as she came quietly into the lofty room and discovered her great-niece, Laura, who, instead of ticking off the numerous items on her list, was standing still, staring solemnly at a marble bust of Shakespeare, which was housed in the arched alcove set into the library wall.

Laura started at her voice, looked round at her great aunt, then frowned, her eyes unexpectedly sombre.

'You make me sound like a machine, India. I was only thinking about how it used to be in Selby. When I was little, I loved my holidays with you.'

She really wanted to add, I don't know how you can bear to sell, but she didn't, because India knew how she felt already—that it was a crime! In fact, every corner of the place held memories of the past. Just staring at the alcove had taken her back sixteen years!

It wouldn't do to let India know that she was remembering that when it had been curtained, it had been Laura's secret hiding-place, where she'd had her first kiss, one day when she was eight and they were playing Sardines. A surprising memory, which hadn't popped up for years! Laura wondered briefly what had happened to the boy who'd kissed her. She couldn't remember a lot about him, except that he'd been gangly for his age, faintly handsome and horribly earnest about that swift peck on the cheek!

Luckily, Laura didn't have to bother with men too much these days. It wasn't because she didn't know any—she'd had several boyfriends—but no-one serious. The fact was, she was far too busy.

'Not a machine, Laura, but rather too wrapped up in your work. You should enjoy yourself more.'

India's eyes were twinkling. Laura's great aunt was a dear and extremely perceptive. That's why it was so surprising that she was determined to sell such a beautiful house as Selby. It meant so much to their family and it was such a shame. Laura was sure that she'd regret her decision.

'I enjoy my work,' she remonstrated.

It was quite true. She loved her job, even though Nick could be a pain sometimes. Laura frowned again.

'You'll get wrinkles like me if you keep on doing that.'

Aunt India was still smiling in a rather mysterious way.

'You haven't any,' Laura retorted then, noticing India's quizzical glance, added, 'Well, not many anyway. You always look the same to me. No older.'

It was true. India's hair was still abundant and softened by low lights. She'd kept her extremely elegant figure and took care with her make-up. Although she was past sixty, she looked ten years younger.

'Thank you, dear, but I'm feeling my age every day,' India replied gently, looking round the library.

She sighed. Selby Hall was really far too big for her to live in on her own. She could see that Laura was about to try to persuade her to change her mind again.

'No, dear, my mind is quite made up about the sale.'

She noticed with a pang that her usually unruffled niece had the hint of a tear in her eye. It certainly wasn't like Laura to be so sentimental over bricks and mortar, given how many houses had passed through her hands recently. Deep inside, India knew that selling Selby had been bound to have an effect on her niece. But she had her own good reasons to press on with the sale!

'I'm sorry,' India said simply, touching her niece's arm lightly.

'I know, but I still don't understand,' Laura replied, wondering for the umpteenth time how India could give up Selby and take on a tiny flat in London.

She, herself, would have been delighted to do just the opposite. At twenty-six, she was becoming a little tired of the city. Taking over as mistress of Selby had always been a totally impractical dream. India didn't want to keep it on and Laura couldn't possibly afford to. She had always promised herself she would make her own breaks.

When she was travelling in South America and helping out at an orphanage in her gap year, she'd often thought about Selby and her own privileged childhood. She used to try to imagine how the poor street children she was helping would react if they saw the place. She'd been so lucky and she was determined to give something back in the end. And she'd do it. How, she wasn't quite sure yet, but it would probably be by donations rather than actions. Time was what she was short of.

Her brother, Sam, had no aspirations in that direction. All he cared about at present was long-haul travelling.

'In spite of all the reasons you've given me over the last few months, I think it's a shame.' She sighed. 'Anyway, at least Quinton's will do their best for you.'

That was something she would make sure of.

Looking down, she tried to concentrate on the work in hand, and the reason she had been walking round the library, slapping numbers on things. She was working on the complicated inventory she was making for her boss, Nick Quinton, who was handling the sale.

'I hope so.'

It had always been India's private opinion that Laura was a sweet girl underneath her efficient exterior, although she had gathered from her recent dealings with some of Laura's colleagues at Quinton Holdings that her niece could be very much the hard-nosed negotiator when it came to business.

Luckily, Laura didn't show that side to her aunt too often, but she certainly looked the part that day in her severe, classically-tailored dark suit and impeccable white silk shirt, an outfit only lightened by that shining halo of totally-natural rich auburn hair, now carefully put up in a smooth chignon, but which, as a child, had cascaded over her shoulders and been the subject of much exclaiming from fond admirers, ever since they had leaned over Laura in her pram.

She had been a beautiful baby, who had grown into an accomplished, young woman. India had great admiration for any girl who could hold her own in a man's world. In India's day, there had been less opportunity.

The world, at present, was Laura's. She'd fought hard for her position in it and there was no way she was going to go down. At present, she was very much up, and an important sale likc Selby Hall was helping her reputation even more, not that it would do to remind her of it. Although she had been born with a silver spoon, she had gone to great lengths to shake off her aristocratic background.

In fact, in her gap year and after taking her degree, she had disappeared for a year each time to South America to work with street children. Once she was back and all the better for her experiences, she had set to make a name for herself in the precious world of fine art. Laura never talked much about her trips but India knew that, quietly, she was still fund-raising for the kids she had left behind.

However, Lady Melling also knew that Laura's boss, Nick Quinton, had an eye to the main chance when he gave her the job buying and selling with Quinton Holdings, as well as being his right-hand woman in auctioneering and real estate. India was not keen on the too-suave Nick. He was a smooth operator, who realised Laura's worth and, especially, her contacts. India's mother, who had been an outspoken Thirties' flapper, would have called him a lounge lizard. Lady Melling wasn't sure what modern term would be applied to Mr Quinton, but she suspected it would be scarcely complimentary!

One thing she was certain of was that Laura wasn't unaware of the fact of how her boss seemed to be using her. At least, India assumed he paid her very well and, above all, she was sure her niece was her own woman.

'Are you going to make a list of all the books as well?' she asked as Laura peered through the glass at her family's lifetime collections.

'No. Someone else is coming in for that,'

Laura replied. 'The British Library was on to me a couple of weeks ago. They're interested in the collection and are sending a specialist, someone called Fiona Wilcox. Goodness, she's due here in the next couple of days. Oh, look,' Laura cried, pointing to a shelf, 'I remember that one! Alice In Wonderland! It was my favourite, with all those lovely pictures. You used to get it out for me and I sat over there!'

Suddenly Laura's heart skipped uncomfortably. What was the matter with her? She was being so unprofessional. India stretched up, unlocked the case and took down the book. She handed it to Laura, who began to turn the pages reverently.

'You naughty girl,' she said, looking over Laura's shoulder. 'Did you try and colour that picture in?'

The Queen of Hearts was a garish purple!

'I'm afraid I did,' Laura confessed. 'By the look of it, when I was about six. Sorry!'

'Well, you better have it then,' India remarked casually, although she was feeling far from casual.

In the end, Laura was going to inherit her money but there was absolutely no way, physically, India could keep this house going. She hadn't told Laura that she was not in good health. It was best to be done with it once and for all. It would have been different if she had had her own children to carry it on. Maybe she could have kept a wing then, while one of

7

them lived in the other part, but it was not to be and she had hatched her plans very carefully.

Laura and her brother, Sam, would share the proceeds when her will was read, but neither knew about the extent of their inheritance yet. Things might have been different if Laura or Sam had married, but the way matters were going that was very unlikely. Sam was wandering somewhere through Nepal and according to Laura, she had no plans whatsoever to settle down!

Laura stared at Alice's cover from which the White Rabbit's anxious eyes gazed. Tears started in her eyes again.

'Thank you,' she said. 'It's lovely. I'll treasure it. I do wish I had the room to take all of the books, but it's quite impossible! India,' she went on, 'I really wish you weren't going through with this sale. You have Mrs Keyes to help you. She's a housekeeper in a million and there are the girls from the village. I'm sure you'll hate it in town!'

India shook her head.

'The books will find a good home, but you must choose what you want before Miss Wilcox arrives.' She sighed once more. 'I'm getting on for seventy, Laura, and I'm miles away from everything stuck here in the backwoods of Herefordshire. It was wonderful when I was thirty, when I had the horses and all my friends were hale and hearty. Besides, I live in dread of someone breaking in. Don't let's go over it all again, please. I've quite made up my mind. I've got a lovely little flat, quite luxurious in fact, and so close to everything. I'm very lucky to have discovered it. I shall be able to go to the theatre when I want, Harrods, Dickins & Jones. I shall love it.'

'If you say so,' Laura replied doubtfully.

Just then, her mobile phone rang. She took out the tiny phone and put it to her ear. During the conversation, India sat down at the table and closed her eyes. She felt extremely tired.

'Who was it?' she asked when Laura finished.

'Nick. He's just left. He doesn't sound in a very good mood though. I can't think why because he just told me he's found a buyer who seems serious about Selby.'

She grimaced. She hadn't expected the news so soon.

'Wonderful!' her aunt said enthusiastically.

Laura glanced at India. Did she really want to give all this up? Laura could still hardly believe it, in spite of her protestations.

'I suppose I'd better get on,' Laura added. 'I promised I'd have at least half of this inventory done, so the Fine Art catalogue can go to press. It's going to be an awfully important sale.'

'Good,' India said. 'All the more for the

coffers.'

But her smile didn't quite reach her eyes, and Laura had noticed. She got up and winced. Her illness was plaguing her today.

'I'd better go and alert Mrs Keyes. Nick'll be famished after driving down from London.'

'Nick is never hungry,' Laura replied. 'He picks. I wouldn't worry about him, if I were you. I don't!'

CHAPTER TWO

The Blue Dining-Room at Selby, with its delicately-sprigged duck-egg blue eighteenth-century decor and its collection of Chinese porcelain in original walnut show cases, had never seemed more beautiful to Laura, now that she was going to lose it, and Nick had never seemed so jaded.

As she looked across the table at his world-weary face and blank eyes as he toyed with his food, she realised that she'd had enough of working for him. Now she was more experienced, she knew that taking the job with Nick had been a mistake, although she enjoyed the work and he paid her a fantastic salary. The main problem was that he was continually intimating that he wanted to get to know her better.

There was absolutely no way that Laura would let herself become romantically involved with her boss. Besides, he already had a girlfriend. Laura had no illusions about Nick and his ambitions. He would do anything to get what he wanted, but Laura was not on offer and she'd made that perfectly clear. Of course, she couldn't hand in her notice right away, but she was going to as soon as she'd settled India's affairs.

As she leaned forward and picked up her

wine glass, the light from the Georgian silver candelabra shed an enchanting glow upon her shining auburn head and the off-the-shoulder aquamarine silk dress she was wearing. She wished she hadn't worn the dress now even though it suited her. There was something in Nick's eyes that she didn't like. She hoped that India hadn't noticed the attention he was paying her.

'Penny for them!' Nick quipped.

Laura came to with a start. He had a questioning look on his face, while India, resplendent in a black and gold embroidered stole, was staring at her quizzically.

'Oh, they were hardly worth that,' she returned quickly.

'What were you thinking of, dear?' India asked.

The answer had to be 'no more real dinner parties'! She glanced across at the portrait of her grandfather, which took pride of place in the Blue Dining-Room, and thought for the hundredth time how exceptionally disagreeable he looked, as he surely would have been had he known that his recalcitrant granddaughter was about to throw Selby Hall to the wolves, one in particular!

'Not a great deal except,' Laura replied, 'except how much I like this room. It's beautiful.'

She finished with a meaningful look at her aunt, which asked plainly, how could she bear to give it all up?

'Sure is,' Nick said, his gaze swivelling around, then leaning back in his chair as comfortably as if he owned the place already.

Coldly, India regarded the newest wolf who was about to save Laura's inheritance. He was dressed in a fashionable suit that looked as if it had just walked itself out of a Mayfair tailor's. His hair was glossy and flicked over his brow carelessly, while his air was faintly languid. Quinton was not a man India could ever have cared for and she certainly didn't like the look that he was giving her niece at that moment, as if he owned her, or wanted to! Suddenly, she was determined to find out if Nicholas Quinton had romantic designs on Laura, and, if he had, to do something about it!

'I'm glad you think so, Mr Quinton,' India interposed, realising that Laura didn't want to voice what she'd been thinking either. 'It's a wonderful house which has served our family well for generations!'

Laura frowned as Nick sat up and began to look interested. She had heard that brittle tone before, which was reserved for people India didn't like. Maybe she was about to relent. Perhaps she'd decided to withdraw Selby from sale after all. But her heart sank as her aunt went on.

'I assume you'll be able to clinch the deal soon. I don't intend to lose the London flat.'

'Nothing to worry about,' Nick replied confidently, his eyes swivelling back to Laura. 'As I told Laura, we have a rather big fish on the hook.'

'Then I think you should let me in on it, Mr Quinton,' India said acidly. A satisfied Laura saw Nick wince.

'Which was what I was about to do, Lady Melling,' Nick replied levelly.

'Who is it?' Laura asked, twirling her wine glass again to cover the misery she was feeling.

'O'Neill Developments!'

'A development company?'

Laura swallowed. Although the wine was the best, the taste in her mouth had suddenly turned sour. Nick was nodding as though he'd presented them both with the best prize in the world. Laura's stomach turned violently at the thought of Selby being sold off for development. She'd seen it happen to so many glorious houses and the idea was preposterous, but she could do nothing about it. It was not her decision, only India's, who was sitting back in her chair now, looking quite white, her long, elegant fingers fiddling with the fine linen napkin. It was the first time Laura had ever thought India looked old, and it shocked her.

'Do you think they'll want to turn it into flats?' Laura asked.

She was being brutal on purpose, twisting the knife, which might be the only way to bring

14

India to her senses. Her aunt couldn't want dear old Selby to end up as a group of luxury apartments!

'Possibly,' Nick replied carefully, realising he was skating on thin ice. 'But it'll be better for you, Lady Melling. It'll bump up the price, of course!'

Laura knew that all Nick was interested in was money. She'd always known that and she had never seen her job with him as anything but temporary. She despised him and all he stood for. She might look like a hypocrite working for him, but it was only a means to an end.

'I see,' India said slowly. 'O'Neill Developments . . . what do you know about the firm?'

'Rock solid,' Nick replied. 'Good reputation but there are others as good on the market.'

Laura shot him a quick glance. What was he up to? First he was telling Aunt India this company was the best and then intimating others might come in, too.

'I think I've heard of it,' India added surprisingly.

'Have you?' Laura asked, puzzled.

'Who is the managing director?' was India's next question, putting Nick on the spot.

'Jack O'Neill. Whizz kid, only thirty. Arrogant guy, but he knows what he's doing in development. He's taken a lot of crumbling, old ruins and transformed them.'

Laura blazed inside at Nick's insensitivity. 'And that's what he intends for here?' she interposed. 'For goodness' sake!' She couldn't contain herself any longer. 'That's not what you want for Selby is it, India? Oh, I'm sorry!' India's face was set.

'Would you like some dessert, Mr Quinton?' she asked, looking under the silver-platter cover. 'It's Mrs Keye's speciality, a kind of Baked Alaska, excellent to cool one down.'

Laura took the hint. Of course, India wouldn't want any hostility she felt about the deal to be aired in front of Nick.

'No ice-cream for me, thank you,' Nick replied. 'I have to look after my figure.'

'What a pity,' India said scathingly. 'That means we'll have to eat it all, dear,' she added, lifting the heavy, Georgian silver knife.

'By the way,' Nick said, watching her ladling out a portion, 'I hope I'm not out of order, but I've made an appointment for O'Neill to came over in the next few days. He's very keen, but I wanted to check it with you first.'

'Thank you for your concern, Mr Quinton,' India said dryly. 'I'd like all the details so I can read up on O'Neill Developments for myself.'

'Fine,' Nick replied, throwing a puzzled glance at Laura, who was just as mystified.

However, Laura knew Aunt India a great deal better than he did. She had something up her sleeve and Laura was praying that the idea

16

of selling to a development company was the last thing India intended for Selby Hall.

CHAPTER THREE

Later that evening, Laura and Nick were seated in the library going over the inventories. Laura hadn't changed, only slipped a warm cashmere cardigan over the aquamarine dress. She was glad she had, because she hadn't liked the way Nick's eyes had roved over her bare shoulders. It made her feel like he was undressing her! But she didn't want to think about that.

Once again, Laura's mind kept flicking back to the past, which wasn't like her as she was paid to concentrate on her work, but she just couldn't help it. The memories of those long-ago childish parties were filling her head, together with other pictures of family get-togethers at Christmas, when they came over to spend the holiday with Aunt India. She recalled her father sitting on the leather Chesterfield, reading his newspaper, and her mother coming over and airily kissing the top of his bald head, while Sam lay playing on the floor with some horrible, noisy toy.

Now her parents were both gone and Sam was thousands of miles away. They'd all been so happy together. To her horror, she could feel tears pricking against her eyelids. Then she was conscious that Nick was looking at her very strangely. She composed herself. She was not going to let him see how upset she was. He was the last man who would understand what she was feeling.

'We're not getting very far, are we, Laura?' he said.

'What do you mean? I think we're doing very well,' Laura replied hesitatingly, knowing perfectly well what he meant.

'I know you're unhappy about this sale,' he said suddenly.

She shot him a quick glance. It was not like him to be sensitive, neither was he given to hesitation. She breathed in quickly, knowing instinctively that something was coming she didn't want to hear. A moment later, his hand slipped over hers and patted it sympathetically. Laura froze.

'There could be a way out for you,' he said conspiratorially.

'And what might that be?' she asked, staring at the lists in front of her where the figures kept dancing in front of her eyes.

'We should get together,' he declared, leaning forward.

'Get together?' she repeated. 'Whatever do you mean?'

'You know perfectly well what I mean. I can rcad you like a book.'

'I don't think so,' she replied icily.

'I'm very fond of you, Laura.'

'Please, Nick!'

'No, listen. What I'm saying is, you and your

brother will inherit this place when your aunt dies. All of it! If you and I got together, well, I'm sure that your aunt would relent. We could live here. She wouldn't have to move. I could commute and you could back me up. Between us, we could afford to keep the place going! You know I'm comfortably off. We could run the business from here together!'

'Are you proposing to me?' she flashed, amazed at his nerve.

'In a manner of speaking. We'd make a good team and I adore you.'

Laura was up on her feet.

'This is ridiculous! Unbelievable!'

'Oh, dear,' he replied calmly. 'I take it the answer's no.' He looked up at her. 'Am I that repulsive?'

'For goodness' sake, Nick, I work for you, that's all. I have no intention of living with or marrying someone I don't love. In any case, you have a girlfriend, or have you forgotten her?'

'She'd soon find someone else,' he shrugged off, sighing. 'Well, I can see I've made a mistake. Forget it. I thought it might solve your problem.'

Laura regarded him with amazement. She'd always known that he'd do anything to get his own way, but this really was the end of their business relationship. How dare he!

'I shan't forget what you've said,' she replied coldly. 'In fact, this might be a good time to inform you about something I've been thinking for a long time. When the sale of Selby is concluded, I intend to hand in my notice.'

He grimaced.

'Ah, well, I suppose I had it coming. I gambled and I lost,' he replied calmly. 'What will you do?'

'That's not your concern,' Laura snapped, gathering her papers and snapping them into her briefcase. 'And I've done about all I intend to do on this tonight!'

'OK.'

He seemed to be taking it all very calmly. She couldn't believe his cheek.

'And please, remember that ours is an entirely business arrangement as it always has been.'

'Pity. We would have made a good team, you know,' he dared. 'And you wouldn't have lost all this!' he added.

With an angry glance that warned him not to speak another word, a flushed Laura stalked out of the library. Once outside the door, she leaned against it and bit her lip to contain her anger.

'The creep,' she said. 'The utter, utter creep!'

She was amazed at Nick's mentality and wished she'd added that this was the 21st century not the Middle Ages when women were married off and became chattels of their husbands. She was an heiress but when she married, it would be because she loved someone, and it would not be Nick Quinton! She walked along several corridors, trying to control herself, stopping a couple of times only to stare blankly out of a window.

'Laura, whatever is the matter?' her aunt asked, coming up silently behind her.

Laura turned and a surprised India saw tears starting in her niece's eyes.

'Nothing very much,' she said, pursing her lips.

'It doesn't seem like nothing,' India replied, stretching out a comforting hand and rubbing Laura's arm to console her. 'Can't you tell me, dear?'

'I'm sorry, India, but, no, I can't, just at the moment,' Laura replied, wiping away the tear that had stubbornly resisted her attempt to control it and had rolled halfway down her cheek. 'I'm all right now, I really am!'

'You know, Laura, I haven't seen you cry for years,' India said softly.

'I'm being silly,' Laura said. 'I think that the sale has got to me at last.'

'I'm sorry, dear, but my mind's made up. There is no way that I can keep Selby on. You know that.'

Laura nodded.

'I know.'

What would India say if she'd told her what Nick had suggested? That if she did what Nick wanted, then Selby would be saved. But she couldn't marry him, or live with him, or have anything to do with him like that, not even for Selby! She sighed, turned and patted her briefcase.

'Well, I suppose I ought to get on with this. I should go over these lists in bed. The printer's waiting for them.'

Laura couldn't resist ramming the point home. It was very nearly India's last chance. The first sale catalogue of the furniture was out already and they'd had enormous interest.

'No! It's far too late to do anything else. You're tired out. You should go to bed to sleep. Anyway, what's the matter with Mr Quinton? He had a face like thunder when I looked into the library. Did you have words?'

'Yes,' Laura replied briefly. 'But I don't want to talk about it.'

'Fine.'

They walked on down the corridor and turned into what India called the snug. Even though it was smaller than many of the other rooms in Selby, it was still a gracious room with a high ceiling and lofty dimensions. Instead of oil paintings, the room had some pretty watercolours, the fireplace was small rather than grandiose and two lovely standard lamps shed a welcoming glow. India spent a great deal of her time in there now because it looked out over the parkland and the stables, which reminded her of her beloved horses. She'd had a small kitchen attached in what had been the dressing-room. A moment later, she was putting on the kettle.

'Hot chocolate?' she called.

'Yes, please,' Laura returned.

She leaned back in the comfortable, winged armchair and tried to decide what she should do next. She couldn't hand in her notice immediately because she wanted to keep an eye on what was going on with Selby. But she didn't know how she was going to work with Nick any more, not after tonight's fiasco.

India came back in and handed her the steaming mug of delicious dark liquid. Laura savoured the smell.

'No-one makes a hot chocolate like you do, India.'

'Thank you, dear. Now,' her aunt replied, sitting down, 'this is the last time I'm going to bring up the subject.'

Laura was looking at her with agonised eyes.

'I can see that you and Nick Quinton do not get on. Why don't you give in your notice?'

Laura stared and a faint smile played round her mouth.

'You're a witch, India! I was just debating that question, but I don't want to leave until the sale goes through.'

'Very sensible,' India replied, thinking on her feet. 'So, if you can bear it, imagine you're working for me rather than him.'

'I was doing that anyway.'

'You mean, he might be crooked!' India exploded.

'No! Not that. He'll do a good job. Besides, the more he gets for Selby, the more he'll make. You know that. His commission is huge.'

Laura had managed to get Nick to quote a slightly lesser price, but only slightly, whereas she was doing it out of love, for India and Selby. What was the price of love? Nick Quinton wouldn't be able to answer that question! She wasn't prepared for what came next.

'After dinner, I looked up O'Neill Developments,' India announced, 'on the Internet. It's a very interesting firm. Maybe it wouldn't be a bad thing if O'Neill's took this place over.'

'Oh, it would!' Laura interposed. 'It would be turned into apartments. Of course, they'd say that they were keeping the character of the place but, India, I've seen other places that have been renovated and they're soulless.'

'Well, I saw some pictures of other places they've done up on their website and they didn't look bad to me.'

Laura could see that it was no use arguing with India when her mind was made up. She might just as well give in and face the inevitable.

'You know what else I noticed?' India added.

'I have no idea,' Laura returned tensely.

'They have an Opportunities Site.'

'What?'

'I clicked on the link and found that Jack O'Neill, you know, the dynamic managing director, is looking for a personal assistant with experience.'

Laura stared at her aunt.

'What are you getting at, India?'

'I think you should apply. The salary is excellent and if he was truly interested in Selby, and if you got the job, you could keep an eye on things as they progress and, then they mightn't be soulless.'

Laura was dumbstruck as India pulled a piece of paper out of her handbag.

'Here, I downloaded the application form!'

Laura stared in disbelief.

'But, I . . .'

'Have a look at what's offered. Look at that salary! I don't know how much Quinton's pay you, but I bet this is more.'

Laura was astounded. What was India up to? Did she really want Selby to be turned into apartments? India's eyes sparkled mischievously as she settled down with her chocolate.

'By the way, when I looked into the library, Mr Quinton wasn't too happy. Have you upset him?'

'Yes, and he'll be a lot more upset if I fill this in,' Laura replied, placing the offending form face downwards on the coffee table.

Half an hour later, when India had gone to bed, leaving her niece to switch off the lights, Laura retrieved the papers, stuffed them into her briefcase and took them with her up to her bedroom.

CHAPTER FOUR

Laura had woken up dejected and lay staring up at the ceiling for ages but, finally, she'd dragged herself out of bed, belted her robe around her and walked over to the window-seat of the bay window of her bedroom.

Looking out over the park, she thought that whatever happened to Selby Hall in the future it would always be the most wonderful place to wake up in early in the morning. A beautiful pheasant was ambling across the lawn below her, followed by his plainer mate, who was jerking her head up and down nervously. They were making for the woods. That's what Laura was going to do, she decided, get outside and clear her head. Her spirits lifted.

She'd always been fond of walking and riding when no-one else was awake. It gave her time to think and, that morning, she needed that more than ever. Undoing her robe, she walked over to the bathroom, glancing across as she did so at the completed application form lying on the desk on the other side of the room. She'd spent too long filling it in last night, that was why she was so tired! She ought to have taken India's advice and gone straight to bed! She'd even placed it in the envelope, addressed it to Jack O'Neill personally, and sealed it.

Laura usually thought about important things for a day or so before acting on them. The form had been completed quickly on account of last night's confrontation with Nick, but, now, she wasn't sure whether she was going to send it off or not. It was a very big step to take, but what India had said about her keeping an eye on the place made sense.

Half an hour later, Laura was taking a leisurely stroll, making for the old stables. How she loved the place where India had kept her horses, but now the horses were gone. Memories of Pole Star jigged around in her head. He'd been a fat, disagreeable white pony, with a habit of turning and nipping his rider's feet. Laura couldn't help smiling at the thought. Sam's pony hadn't been quite as naughty. Later on, both of them had graduated to full-height horses and had ridden all through their school holidays. Halcyon days, never to be repeated! Things can't stay the same for ever, the little voice in Laura's head reminded, but it didn't help a bit.

Laura walked along the gravel path towards the stables where a handsome Georgian archway led into a courtyard. She noted that the arch wasn't as well kept now as it had been. Strands of ivy were hanging down and some of the brickwork was crumbling. Doubtless the new owners would have to do something about that. The stables would probably end up as garages for the wealthy

29

owners' fancy limousines.

She gasped as she walked through the arch and saw the magnificent sports car parked against the red-brick wall. It was a sleek soft-top Mercedes! What was it doing in her stables? There was no sign of life. Where was its owner? She peered through the windows. On the seat lay an expensive leather tan briefcase and a touring map. Whoever it belonged to evidently wasn't worried about it being broken into. On the passenger seat, a woman's pink pashmina was folded and, under it, the corner of what Laura recognised as the Selby furniture catalogue.

'What a cheek!' Laura said out loud.

The trespasser must have been having a nose round before the sale, but how had he or she got through the remote-controlled gates at the bottom of the drive? Laura frowned and took out her mobile phone. Then she realised that it was only six forty-five and she couldn't possibly ring Mrs Keyes at that hour, even though she'd been with India so many years that she would understand Laura's anxiety. Anyway, she was probably in the shower. Her husband, Ken, was the handyman-cum-gardener-cum-everything and he certainly would still be in bed.

Maybe she should ring the police, but the nearby village had no station and they'd have to send a car from Hereford, which was fifteen miles away. She could imagine what they'd say, that's if they ever turned up!

No, she'd have to investigate for herself. Maybe it was one of Nick's friends, or one of the Quinton clients. Laura bristled. If it was, how dare he not tell her. Suddenly, she was convinced that was the answer. Nick had probably given someone prior permission to look round before the sale.

Laura walked out of the courtyard when she'd satisfied herself that all the stable buildings were empty. She stood beside the arch, looking up to the path that disappeared into the woods. It would be very silly to go up there, only asking for trouble, the little voice in her head insisted. Nevertheless, Laura walked slowly towards where the path began. It sloped upwards, steeply, narrowing as it climbed. She knew the view through the trees was tremendous. On a clear day, the Black Mountains could be seen, overshadowing the distant landscape. The sun was well up now and Laura longed to see again the landscape she'd always loved.

How many times had she ridden up there as a teenager to meet Martyn, her first love, who went to the local comprehensive and whom she was only able to see in the holidays from boarding school! Laura smiled to herself. She used to sneak off up there on her horse, tether it to a branch and wait for him. Her father would have gone mad if he'd known.

Now, in spite of her misgivings, Laura was

already climbing up again! She left the path and searched for the fallen tree which had been felled by lightning. It was a wonderful seat for a breather. She yawned, tired out after a bad night, staring across the countryside. The view was as it had always been, a patchwork landscape of green and yellow, bordered by untidy little hedges, sweeping crazily down to the silver river.

'I'll never see this again,' she said out loud, and jumped up from her seat as an unmistakable cough echoed below her!

Startled, she saw the top of the man's head—the trespasser! He was standing about three metres below, leaning precariously against a tree. Below, the slope rolled down a sheer fifty metres. He must be crazy!

'What are you doing?' she called tersely.

Laura could be brittle when she wanted to and her tone was enough for the man to swing round and look up. She found herself staring down into the darkest eyes she had ever seen, large and luminous. She bristled.

'Who are you? Do you know you're trespassing?'

He frowned, making his smooth, tanned brow into a broad furrow. He had a deep tan which proclaimed he was well-travelled and used to wintering in hot climates.

'No, I didn't,' he called up nonchalantly without any hint of regret.

She saw his mouth working and knew

instinctively he was suppressing a grin. That was too much for Laura. Not only was he unrepentant, he was mocking her. He was also immensely handsome. They stared at each other, then suddenly he shot up an arm and caught hold of a stout branch above him. Balancing easily, he slipped his hand into the pocket of his designer jeans, pulled out an object and waved what Laura immediately recognised as the box-like device to open the gates!

'How did you get that?' she added. 'This is private property!'

He replaced it in his pocket and, next moment, let go of the branch and began leaping up the slope. Anyone else would have scrambled! Laura took two indignant steps back as he landed beside her and began to brush the mud off his fashionable jacket.

'And you are?'

Close to, she could see that his eyes were full of fun. He straightened.

'It doesn't matter!' she challenged, facing him.

He was standing very close now. He was much taller than she was, at least six foot two, wearing an open-necked shirt under his jacket.

'It does,' he said. 'I always like to know who's about to beat me up.'

The grin broke out and Laura realised that he was devastatingly handsome when he smiled. She looked away.

'Don't be ridiculous.'

'Well,' he replied, 'if we're going to continue to play games . . .'

'Games! I'm not playing games. You're trespassing,' she snapped. 'I'm Lady Melling's niece and this is private property.'

'Not for long,' he said, turning to survey the view. 'Fantastic, isn't it? One of the best landscapes I've seen, and I've seen a few! But I'm afraid there'll be people crawling all over soon.' He turned back. 'Pity! If this was my place, I wouldn't let it go.'

The atmosphere was full of tension as they regarded each other. 'How dare you? My aunt has her reasons for selling.'

What was she doing even talking to him? She had no intention of discussing family business with a total stranger. Laura bit her lip.

'You have no right to be up here,' she reiterated. 'I was about to call the police,' she added as an afterthought.

'Well, I'd be all right if you had, because I collected the gate key from the agent.' He shrugged. 'Guess that's OK with you, is it, or do you own the agency as well?'

Laura choked. He was looking at her as if he wanted to know her better. The man was insufferable.

'No! But I work for it. I'm Nick Quinton's personal assistant!' she exploded.

'Tut, tut,' he replied annoyingly.

34

He thought she wasn't on the ball, that she wasn't doing her job properly! Laura could have killed him!

'Tell me who you are!'

It was an order rather than a plea. The man had mischief written all over his face. He also had the nerve to refuse.

'I suggest you ask your boss, but off the record, I work for O'Neill's. It's a good firm that can spot a real treasure, and this sure is one.'

It was the first time she'd heard a hint of American in his accent.

'Well,' he added, shaking his head, 'I've had my fill of the view, and the atmosphere. On both counts, it's magnificent.'

She knew what he meant. How dare he pay her such an unwelcome compliment? Laura wanted to kick back, to scream at him that the place wouldn't be magnificent when O'Neill Developments had ruined it but, luckily, she had more sense and dignity. He yawned suddenly, then glancing at his watch, quipped, 'It's really early, isn't it? Do you often walk round your estate at this time of the morning?'

'Very often,' Laura responded grimly. 'One never knows whom one is going to meet.'

'Oh, yes, trespassers. I'm glad you didn't have the guard dogs with you.'

'Please, go away,' she said.

She felt entirely confused. She should have snapped his head off instead of playing his game, but there was something else in his eyes, a softness that told her he was probably sorry for his behaviour but she could see that he wasn't the kind of man to own up to the slightest weakness.

'OK,' he said, putting up his hands in a mocking gesture. 'Thank you for letting me look at your view. I'm sure we'll meet again before the sale.'

'Perhaps,' Laura said icily, wishing she could add, I hope not, but it wouldn't have been sensible to insult a potential buyer.

'Goodbye.'

He was still grinning. She watched him walk off down the path, with an effervescent energy that showed his total fitness. She felt her eyes focus on his back, taking in every lithe contour, remembering that devilishly-handsome face crowned with fashionably-cut hair. Well, if he was an advertisement for O'Neill's, then Selby was doomed.

The man had probably been chosen by the company, not only for his charm, but his business acumen as well. He was a total package, one of the hawks. He'd show no mercy. Then she thought of the application form that she'd been foolish enough to fill in. No way would she work for a firm who employed someone like that. She might have to work with him!

Suddenly, Laura felt entirely miserable. The morning sun had also disappeared behind what seemed to be hovering rain clouds, so, finding no enthusiasm for her own walk any longer, she turned back down the slope, too. As she did so, she heard the distant thunder of the car engine as he took off down the drive beneath her. Strangely, the folded pashmina on the passenger seat came suddenly into her mind. He evidently had a girlfriend, probably several. He was the kind of man certain girls loved to be with, but not a girl like Laura.

Power was a turn-on, but not at the expense of everything else. She wanted the whole package, too, but of a different kind, someone sweet, who wasn't selfish like Nick; someone with power, which hadn't corrupted him; someone handsome, not vain; good-humoured, not mocking; intelligent, but not arrogant!

Laura had no illusions. Her perfect man didn't exist. Well, she hadn't met him yet anyway. She sighed as she walked past the stables. She had to admit that things weren't going too well in her world at the moment. Her plans to put India off the sale had failed. Nick had totally the wrong idea about the relationship that existed between them, making her job untenable, and the brash messenger sent by his important buyer had made her feel utterly miserable.

'Oh, what's happening to me? To us all?' she said out loud as, fifteen minutes later, she left the woods and walked back into the house to find India taking her breakfast in the snug.

Her aunt looked pale and tired, as worn-out as Laura felt. She'd evidently had a bad night, too. India had always been a morning person, smartly-dressed and habitually finishing her breakfast by eight. However, this morning she was still wearing her dressing-gown.

Her aunt indicated the table, which was laid for breakfast.

'You look fed-up, Laura,' she said. 'Would you like a piece of toast?'

Laura sat down.

'Have you had any breakfast?'

She shook her head. At that moment, she wanted to be mothered, and her aunt was the one to do it. She always had. Suddenly it struck Laura how much she owed India.

'That's bad for you,' India added, handing over the toast rack.

Morosely, Laura spread butter on to a triangle and covered it with India's best marmalade. That had always cheered her up.

'Good,' her aunt said leaning back. 'Now where have you been this time in the morning? Couldn't you sleep?'

'I went as far as the stables and then for a walk in the woods.'

'Well, it doesn't seem to have cheered you up much.'

'It didn't,' Laura said. 'In fact, just the opposite.'

'Why what happened?'

'Well . . .'

Laura hadn't been going to say anything about the stranger but she couldn't help it. Her mind was full of him.

'I met the rudest man.'

'My dear!' India exclaimed.

'No, not like that. Goodness!' Laura said, wrinkling her brow and smiling in spite of herself. 'I mean, we had words.'

'Well,' India replied, 'who was he? I can't wait.'

'Someone Nick gave the gate keys to!'

'Well, really!'

'When you hear,' Laura added, 'you might be pleased. I don't exactly know who he was, except he worked for O'Neill Developments. He'd had the nerve to come up here, virtually at dawn, and nose around.'

Laura's cheeks were now quite pink.

'He seems to have made an impression,' India observed dryly.

'He certainly did that.'

'Why, what did he say?'

India was determined to find out about the chap who'd managed to rattle her laid-back niece.

'It wasn't what he said, more his attitude. Arrogant, brash, insufferable.' Laura shook her head. 'And he was laughing at me.' She frowned. India was smiling. 'I don't think it's funny. He was trespassing!'

'I'm not laughing at you, dear. I've never

39

known a man get the better of you yet. Was he handsome?'

'What?' Laura asked inelegantly. 'Why?'

'I just had a feeling he might have been.'

'Why?'

'Young, handsome. If he hadn't been, he'd never have taken you on.'

'I don't understand you.'

'Laura, if he'd been middle-aged or elderly, he'd have been dazzled by you, and also quite polite. It's different these days. It's only someone forceful and young who'd spar with you.'

'You've been reading too many magazines, India.'

Laura smiled. She was already feeling better. It was true—he had taken her on and she'd risen to the challenge.

'So he was handsome?'

'Wildly, India, and he was a . . . a pain!'

'I think I have the picture,' India said leaning back. 'I'm getting more interested by the minute. I wonder if O'Neill's will send him again.'

'I hope not,' Laura said. 'But, unfortunately, they probably will. He said they might.'

'Did he?'

India's eyes sparkled. Evidently, her tiredness was wearing off.

'You're awfully naughty, India!' Laura reproved, loving it when her aunt behaved like her best friend.

'I've always liked handsome, young men,' India remonstrated.

'Stop it,' Laura said playfully, then sighed. 'Well, I suppose I ought to go and change. Has Nick appeared yet?'

She wondered what on earth she was going to say to him.

'Yes, and he left you this,' India said and handed her an envelope.

Laura opened it and scanned the contents, conscious of India's questioning eyes. Laura shrugged.

'He's gone back to the office. I'm in charge.'

'And he'd made himself so comfortable. What happened between you two last night?'

Laura breathed in. She might as well come clean.

'He had the nerve to ask me to marry him.'

India looked shocked.

'But it seemed that it was to be a business merger. In fact, he wanted to live here and run the place, with me by his side.'

'The cheek of it!' India exploded.

'That's what I thought last night.'

'You don't mean to say you've changed your mind?' India was aghast.

'I would never marry Nick Quinton if he was the last man on earth.'

'Good,' India said. 'I applaud your taste and your decision. And talking about that, I took the liberty of posting your application form.'

'You didn't!' Laura was shocked.

41

'No, I actually didn't, but I gave it to Keyes, who was going into town.'

'We must get it back!'

India shook her head.

'Oh, dear, I think it's too late. He left at least twenty minutes ago. I told him to put it in the letter-box directly, thinking you'd want it getting there as soon as possible. I am silly, aren't I? As it was sealed and stamped, I thought you'd made up your mind.'

'I had last night but, now . . .' Laura was at a loss for words. It was her own fault. 'Oh, I don't know!'

'I am sorry. Will you forgive me?'

'Yes, of course. It's my own stupid fault. I shouldn't have filled in the blessed thing. I can't imagine how I ever thought I'd want to work for O'Neill Developments.'

'And it's my fault, too.' India looked crestfallen.

'No, no. I mightn't be offered the job. And if I am, I can always refuse.'

'You never know,' India said. 'It mightn't be that bad after all. And you would be able to keep an eye on Selby.'

'I suppose so. Now I really must go and tidy up.'

'Certainly, dear, and, once again, I'm sorry if I did the wrong thing.'

It was not like India to keep apologising. She'd probably made up her mind to post the letter whatever happened. She was as determined as Laura herself, but Laura wouldn't hold it against her. She understood very well that, in spite of what India said about looking forward to living in London, there was no way that she would desert Selby Hall utterly.

Laura slid Nick's note into her pocket. She hadn't told India exactly what he'd said, that he was devastated by both her decisions—not to marry him and to give in her notice. He called it a double blow. Laura knew that wasn't quite true. Nick would shake off his disappointment very quickly but, nevertheless, she was glad he'd gone back to the office as it might have been very difficult working side by side over the next couple of days.

He'd also added that Fiona Wilcox had left a text message to say that she'd be in Selby by lunchtime. As for Jack O'Neill, he was believed to be on his way down, but Nick would let her know further on that one.

'See you later, India,' she said. 'Fiona Wilcox will be here at lunchtime. You know, to look over the books.'

'Yes, dear, I remember.'

India waved Laura out and, as soon as she was sure her niece had gone, withdrew an expensive-looking brochure from under a pile of magazines.

'Ah,' she said, 'now let's have a look at this.'

Putting on her reading glasses and getting out her ballpoint, she opened the glossy folder and stared fixedly at the photograph on the front page.

'Hmmm, extremely handsome,' she said, tapping the young man's face with the end of her pen, 'but I'm not surprised, not at all.'

Then she flipped through the folder, noting points and marking them.

Ten minutes later, she yawned and leaned back in her chair, leaving the O'Neill Developments' glossy brochure open on her knee.

'No, I'm not surprised at all,' she murmured to herself, 'not one little bit.'

Then she closed her eyes.

CHAPTER FIVE

Laura had two more surprises in store that day. First of all, India brought Fiona Wilcox into the library where she was sitting working on the list of the Selby paintings.

The specialist from the British Library was more like a model than a librarian. Sophistication oozed out of her. She was wearing a chic designer suit in silver-grey, with little underneath except the tiniest hint of a lacy bra. Her matching grey shoes were top of the range and her smart, hide briefcase was evidently designer.

'Miss Wilcox, this is my niece, Laura Fenton. She's handling the sale for me,' India said, putting her heavy briefcase down.

'Hello.'

As Fiona shook hands with Laura, her touch was distantly brief, as was her look when her icy-blue eyes scanned the contents of the library.

'Oh, I was led to believe that the collection was rather bigger,' she added, sounding quite put out as she drew some papers out of her briefcase.

Laura was not herself that day. Her week had caught up on her at last and she felt entirely fragile. She was also conscious that what she was wearing was less than smart—a pair of jeans and a plain white shirt under a heavy navy-blue cotton sweater.

'It may not be the biggest collection you've handled, Miss Wilcox, but I'm sure you'll find it of importance.'

Laura saw India glance at her sharply.

'I hope so,' Fiona drawled, looking round once more. 'Is there somewhere I can sit? I'm used to a proper desk.'

'I'm sorry, Miss Wilcox, but the two desks that stood in those alcoves, eighteenth-century French, have been removed for the furniture sale,' India interposed meaningfully.

Laura's eyes narrowed. Who did this girl think she was, requesting a special place to sit? Fiona was looking at the magnificent library table.

'I suppose this will do, but I wonder if it can be moved.'

Laura and India looked at each other doubtfully. It was extremely heavy!

'I'm not being difficult, Lady Melling, but sunlight isn't good for the kind of material I usually work with.'

Fiona sauntered to a spot at the other side of the room.

'Just here would be absolutely right.'

'I'm afraid we can't move it,' India said and Fiona lifted her eyebrows. 'Mr Keyes, my housekeeper's husband, is out, and none of us would be able to manage it. However, Laura and I could fetch a trestle for you out of the utility room.'

If Laura hadn't been feeling so brittle, she would have chuckled at Fiona's expression. The girl had probably never heard of a trestle! She and India left the library and, once they were out of earshot, India burst into laughter.

'What a snob!'

'I can't believe it!' Laura shook her head.

'She's probably used to better things.' India was trying to compose herself. 'Come on, let's fetch the trestle. The quicker we get her started, the quicker she'll be gone. Oh, dear, I wonder what I should give her for lunch.'

'Caviar?' Laura suggested as they hurried down the corridor.

Fiona Wilcox actually did quite well as India cajoled Mrs Keyes into preparing a fresh salmon with a light salad. India had the meal served in the Blue Dining-Room, which happily seemed to go down fairly well in Miss Wilcox's estimation, as did the food. She had an excellent appetite, which belied her fragile exterior. Then the girl returned to her work in the library!

Laura couldn't bear to sit in there with her and watch all the books she'd loved as a child be assessed, analysed and, in some cases, discarded! So she carried on checking off the Fine Art list. She had reached what used to be the hallowed ground of her father's study when she heard the doorbell. She paused and brushed her hair back from her face as it rang again.

Evidently, neither India nor Mrs Keyes had heard. Bother! They must be in the garden, Laura thought, I suppose I'll have to go. I hope it's no-one important. She put her list under her arm, hurried down the corridors and, finally, across the black and white tiled hall. The doorbell rang again!

'For goodness' sake, I'm coming,' she snapped, juggling the list while opening the door then exclaiming, 'You!'

The man she'd met earlier that morning was smiling that same mocking smile, which had made her bristle, searching her face with those dark, expressive eyes. But he was wearing a suit now, of the latest fashion.

'Good afternoon,' he said politely. 'May I come in?'

Laura frowned. He had their brochure in his hand.

'Do you have an appointment?'

'Oh, come on,' he said. 'I did telephone. Honestly!'

'Whom did you telephone?'

She sounded so prim. Just like the maid!

'I telephoned your boss. Didn't you know? Check with him if you like.'

'I shall!'

'Want to do it now? Then I can come in.'

'I believe you.'

She'd meant the sentence to be sarcastic, but he didn't seem to notice. She stepped back. Next moment, he was inside and looking round the gracious hall.

'Very nice. Wonderful, in fact. Does your boss make you do the spring-cleaning as well?'

She was suddenly conscious of how she must look!

'Very funny,' she snapped, about to add that she was cataloguing the pictures for the art collection, but choked it back. Why should she explain herself to him?

'Why are you here?'

He waved the brochure at her.

'O'Neill Developments are very serious about this property and I'm here to report to the board on it. I'd very much like to see over the whole place.'

'I'm sorry, but you need to make a proper appointment.'

The idea of showing him over the house wasn't one she relished, although the appealing look on his face made her relent a little.

'I have. It's just that it wasn't fixed. Mr Quinton knew I was coming, and you're here. What better guide could I find than the niece of the owner?'

'I'm very busy,' she replied.

'Then it'll be a good stress-buster,' he insisted. 'You look all-in.'

At that moment, an alarmed Laura realised that she was warming to his charm. He knew how to treat a woman, that was for sure. But,

49

suddenly, she found herself thinking that it was probably better she took him round rather than Nick. Nick was too pushy and Laura would have the opportunity to sit on the fence. She didn't want O'Neill Developments taking the place over but, on the other hand, if their offer couldn't be resisted then she intended to have her finger right on their pulse, like India wished her to.

'I'm glad you're considering my request,' he added.

'How do you know I am?' she demanded, thinking about the time she'd be wasting when she had to finish what she was doing.

'You said you were busy cataloguing,' he replied, 'so why don't we kill two birds with one stone, so to speak?'

'I don't understand.'

'Bring your work with you. I'm very interested in fine art and I've heard about your pictures.'

'Have you? Where?'

'Oh, I make that kind of thing my business. You'd be surprised at the treasures in some of the old places O'Neill's look at.'

Laura frowned and stared fixedly at her list.

'I wouldn't,' she said. 'Remember, it's my job, and Selby Hall is a very special old place to me. OK, you've talked me into it, but we might have to go slowly through the bedrooms. I've finished with the lower floors.'

'It's OK. I never hurry through bedrooms.'

His roguish eyes twinkled. Laura ignored the quip, but her heart thudded.

'Let's start at the top floor then, shall we?'

As she led him upstairs, he said, 'You don't like me very much, do you?'

'I don't know you,' she said candidly, 'but I admit that I'm not keen on your company taking over Selby Hall.'

'Why?'

'I don't want to see it lose its character. I've spent half my life here and frankly, it's home to me. But I don't want to discuss it. That's for my aunt.'

'And you think O'Neill's would ruin it?' he asked.

She shrugged. Evidently he wasn't expecting an answer because he was examining the balusters of the stairs. She saw with surprise how his hand lingered lovingly on the twisting wood.

'Barley sugar,' he commented. 'I loved it as a kid. They don't make them like that these days.'

A moment later, he was dashing in front of her on to the landing where the two landscapes hung that had been painted by a well-known Irish artist.

'These are Sullivans?'

He was staring at the pictures in admiration.

'Yes,' she answered.

The man was full of surprises. Sullivan was not well known in England.

'How do you know the artist?'

'I work for O'Neill's!' was the cryptic reply.

He was also able to identify nearly all the pictures on the landing and wasn't at all arrogant when Laura had to tell him who'd painted the ones he couldn't put a name to.

Ten minutes later, Laura had begun to enjoy herself, until the little voice in her head reminded her just who she was showing round, one of the men who was about to destroy her heritage!

In the Gentleman's Dressing-Room, he stood looking at the Victorian hip bath and the narrow, tall wash-stand.

'Pity the poor fellow who had to use that,' he remarked and Laura smiled. She'd often thought the same herself.

'My father tried it once. He got stuck!'

She actually giggled at the thought.

'Really?'

He broke into peals of laughter.

'I was only about seven. I just stood and laughed. He was terribly angry.'

'You've a lovely smile,' he said. 'You should use it more!'

Laura was at a loss for words. Seconds later, he was ahead of her again. They dallied in both the south and west bedrooms and he made some knowledgeable remarks about not only the paintings but also the furniture. But when he stood by the 19th-century half-tester bed, fixed her with his hot dark eyes and said,

'Wouldn't mind trying this one!' she had to go over to the window and draw his attention to the view.

They were very close when they stood together by the drapes and she could almost feel the electricity he was sparking off in her. He was a very attractive man! And she'd hated him this morning!

'What's in there?' he asked, pointing to a small doorway next to the bedroom.

'The boudoir.'

'Aren't we going in?' He was extremely close. 'Or am I not allowed?'

'There's not a great deal in there. It used to be my grandmother's personal sitting-room. It's my favourite, so comfy and welcoming.'

'Do you remember your grandmother?'

Laura shook her head.

'Mine was a martinet. But I was a very naughty boy,' he went on.

'I can imagine it,' she said sincerely, crossing to open the door.

The small boudoir was full of afternoon light, which fell on the great, dusty harp, waiting to be collected for the sale. Suddenly, an agonised pang struck her full in the chest. She wouldn't be able to come up here again when she liked, ever, nor see the harp again.

'What's the matter?' he asked, walking over to the instrument and examining it carefully.

She shook her head.

'I used to play that, but I wasn't much good.'

She touched the strings, which quivered. He came back to her side.

'When I was upset, I always came up here and played it.'

'You really don't want to leave this place, do you?'

'No, I don't.' She pressed her lips together.

'I sympathise,' he said. 'Neither would I if it belonged to me.'

'It soon will!' she snapped, recovering, as she knew she was behaving abominably, as though it was her house not India's! 'Please, let's get on.'

The upstairs' tour finished in the Picture Gallery, where the works of Edith Melling were displayed.

'She was a fine artist,' he said, peering closely at the canvas. 'Certainly fits into the Victorian lady mode. You're not selling these, are you?'

'I'm afraid so,' she said, looking at her list, 'as a collection. My aunt would have nowhere to keep them. None of us has.'

'Pity,' he said. 'Let's hope they don't go to an overseas buyer. I like that one particularly.'

'That's not a Melling.'

He lifted his eyebrows.

'I mean, Edith didn't paint it.'

He grinned. She knew he was laughing at her confusion.

'Whoever did paint it captured your aunt perfectly.'

54

She had to agree with him.

'I assume she's taking it with her.'

'No, she's not, but it isn't in the catalogue either. She commissioned it but she didn't like it. He was a young artist and she didn't want to hurt his feelings. That's why it's up here. She says it makes her look ancient. I'm hoping that she won't add it to the sale, even though she says she wants to get rid of it. I'm going to buy it if she does.'

'Good for you!' he said with alacrity.

Laura grimaced. As they went down the three flights to the lower floors, she occasionally felt his hand under her elbow. Each time, it was like an electric current going through her body.

Back in the main hall, she said, 'Well, that's upstairs done. Shall we start in the library? Oh, dear, I almost forgot. We have someone in from the British Library looking over the collections. Perhaps we shouldn't go in there. I could show you the Drawing Room and the Blue Dining Room, and that's the lot really.'

'Thank you,' he said, looking at his watch, 'but time's getting short and I have another appointment. I'd like to come back though another day and finish it off.'

He opened the furniture catalogue and stared at the map on the back. 'There's another room here we haven't seen.'

He pointed to the snug.

'I'm afraid that's private,' Laura said firmly,

knowing India wouldn't appreciate her taking him in there.

'What's private, Laura?' India asked, appearing through the kitchen door.

She was wearing a waxed jacket and wellingtons. She'd evidently been in the garden. She flashed a glance at the visitor and stood completely still.

'The snug. Aunt India, this is the man from O'Neill's. I've been showing him round.'

India looked quite pale.

'Are you all right?' Laura asked her aunt.

'I'm perfectly well, thank you.'

Just then, the library door swung open to reveal Fiona Wilcox.

'Ah,' she called and her face illuminated with a wonderful smile. 'Jack! I was wondering what time you'd make it.'

She hurried over to them.

'Jack?' Laura gasped, flashing him a glance.

'Jack O'Neill, Lady Melling.'

He took India's hand and shook it.

'Miss Fenton, sorry I didn't explain, but we had already met. Hello, Fiona,' he said. 'How's it going?'

'Slowly, darling. I've almost finished for the day. You remember I came in a cab, so you'll be able to give me a lift back to the hotel, won't you?'

Jack nodded.

'Great. I'll just gather my things.'

A moment later, she was stalking off again.

The trio watched her.

'I've enjoyed this afternoon immensely,' Jack said. 'I compliment you on a wonderful house, Lady Melling.'

India inclined her head. She had a very strange look on her face.

'And thank you, Miss Fenton, for showing me round. I'd have a rest, if I were you. You look tired. I'm sure we'll meet again soon.'

He put out his hand and Laura had no option but to take it. His grip was warm, but not comforting.

'I'm sure we will,' she replied acidly.

She was thoroughly confused and exceptionally annoyed. Why hadn't he introduced himself properly? It had been entirely underhand to behave in that way, letting her think that he was an employee. She might have said anything. Then she knew she wouldn't have because, after all, she was very good at her job! She lifted a determined chin.

'But I'd appreciate it if, next time, you make a proper appointment.'

'I definitely will,' he said. 'I love this place. It's enchanting.'

India didn't respond. Why was she behaving so strangely? After all, she was the one who'd been pushing O'Neill's.

'And I'll let Quinton's know that,' he added, 'as well as what a difference a good personal assistant makes. Pity I haven't one as efficient to run my life for me!'

His eyes twinkled, and Laura's heart almost stopped. He couldn't have had the letter yet. She closed her eyes momentarily at the thought of working for him. It would be impossible! Seconds later, a fragile Fiona was standing beside them.

'My bags are in there, Jack,' she said. 'You'll bring them to car? They're frightfully heavy. Thank you so much, Lady Melling. I'll be back tomorrow.'

India exchanged a glance with her niece, who was glowering. Moments later, Jack was shaking hands with Laura again.

'Thank you for a wonderful afternoon,' he said. 'It's been a pleasure to meet you twice!'

'Twice?' India asked, puzzled, as he shook her hand, too.

'I'm afraid I accosted your niece in the woods this morning, Lady Melling, but I'm not really the big, bad wolf I'm cracked up to be!'

They didn't speak as they watched him walk through the door and close it behind him.

'Charming!' India said.

'Too much so!' Laura replied.

'But devastatingly handsome!' India added in a faraway tone.

'If you say so,' Laura retorted, walking off across the hall.

CHAPTER SIX

The following morning, Laura couldn't get Jack O'Neill out of her mind, and India was no help. Her aunt seemed as much taken by him as by the idea of his development company buying Selby.

'I just have a feeling it will be in good hands!' she declared after breakfast.

'I can't see why,' an exasperated Laura replied. 'You looked at their website! They have a habit of buying up large houses and turning them into flats. Is that really what you want?'

'I don't see why not. In fact, if I hadn't made up my mind about taking the place in London, I wouldn't mind staying here in one myself. But it would be far too lonely.'

'India! It would kill you to wake up in the morning and know that you were surrounded by a lot of strangers.'

'Won't it be the same in London?' India asked solemnly.

'No. I won't be far away, and Sam will pop in.'

India looked extremely doubtful, as well she might. As soon as her nephew got home, he got the wanderlust again, just like his father.

'Besides . . .' Laura was about to add, You'll have a wonderful time in London after selling.

All the shops and theatres you want . . . but realised how undiplomatic the remark would be. India had never cared for that kind of life, being happy with her horses and the countryside. That was why Laura couldn't understand her motives.

'I wouldn't want to come down here and see it broken up,' Laura said.

It sounded like she was being selfish, but it would have killed her, too, but maybe she was being selfish.

'You're right,' India said, nodding. 'But, well . . . we'll have to see.'

Laura didn't ask her what that meant because then they heard the door bell ring.

'It's all right, Mrs Keyes will go.'

Fiona Wilcox had arrived on the dot of nine, looking like she'd stepped off the catwalk. When she took off her long camel coat and unwrapped the same pink pashmina that Laura had seen on the seat of Jack O'Neill's Mercedes, the grey suit had been replaced by a perfect white silk blouse and a beautiful, short, navy skirt which revealed a huge amount of glossy, racehorse-like leg!

Fiona yawned behind her hand as she was shown into the library and settled herself down finally after ordering a cup of milky coffee with one sugar and biscuits, cream, if possible. They left her to it again.

'How did she arrive, Mrs Keyes?' Laura asked quietly as she passed the housekeeper

60

on her way upstairs.

'In a taxi, Miss Laura.'

Laura was relieved. So Fiona hadn't enjoyed another lift with Jack O'Neill. She wondered if he would turn up again. Probably not. Then she grimaced as she thought of him opening her letter, but, of course, he wouldn't. His secretary would! It was all so embarrassing.

A couple of hours later when she was settling down for elevenses, her mobile phone rang. It was Nick!

'How are you getting on? We need that catalogue for the printers.'

'I've finished,' she replied. 'You'll have it by tomorrow. Any news on the house sale?'

They were both avoiding anything personal in their conversation.

'O'Neill is keen!'

'Is he?' Her heart missed a beat.

'He's determined to handle the whole thing himself. Goodness knows why when he has a team of estate agents at his disposal. He's going to come down to look round. He phoned me yesterday.'

'Did he?'

'Yes. Watch out for him. He's a cool customer, but he mightn't have it all his own way yet.'

'Why?' Laura frowned. 'Is there someone else interested?'

'Yes. Can't say more at the moment.'

She knew Nick far too well. His tone told

her that he wasn't ready to disclose the new buyer even to her.

'Are they likely to offer more than O'Neill?'

She was imagining Jack O'Neill's response to competition. He probably fought hard!

'It's a possibility, all the better for your aunt. And that's our job, isn't it?'

Nick would have sold his soul to the highest bidder.

'Anyway, watch out for Jack. He'll be round. Keep this under your hat!'

Laura was disgusted. Surely he'd known her long enough to realise that she was the soul of discretion. She put away her mobile thoughtfully. This new buyer put a completely different context on everything. Should she let India know? Of course not. She seemed set on O'Neill having the place. But maybe she'd change her mind if someone offered more. For some strange reason, Laura suddenly hoped that Jack O'Neill liked Selby just as much as he said he did.

Suddenly Laura found herself walking in the direction of the library. Fiona lifted her graceful head as Laura approached. She was examining the first edition of Laura's edition of Alice in Wonderland.

'Good morning.' Her forehead was creased in a frown. 'Did you know, Miss Fenton, that this volume has been vandalised?'

The utter shock in her tone made Laura want to laugh.

'What do you mean?'

'Someone has coloured in several of the plates!'

Laura bent over to look.

'Good heavens,' she said, staring at the garish colours.

She certainly had been a naughty little girl! Fiona put the book aside distastefully on a small pile as if she couldn't bear to touch it.

'Not for us, I'm afraid,' she said.

'That's good,' Laura said, 'because it's mine anyway. It wasn't for sale.'

Fiona looked puzzled.

'My aunt has told me that I can pick out what books I want.'

'She didn't tell me that.'

'I'm sure she will,' Laura replied, smiling and picking up Alice. 'Were you comfortable at the Chesney? I've heard it's quite good.'

'Tolerably.'

Fiona was evidently used to grander places than the best country hotel in the whole of rural Herefordshire.

'Have you known Mr O'Neill long?' Laura asked, wishing she didn't have to, but knowing that she had to find out.

'Jack? Ages.'

'He seems very interested in Selby.'

'Oh, he is.' Fiona looked round. 'It's a lovely old house.' It was the first time that Laura had seen her show enthusiasm for anything. 'Although, and please don't take this amiss, I think it needs a good going-over.'

'What do you mean exactly?' Laura's eyes sparked.

'If Jack bought it, it would be for himself.'

'Himself?'

'Yes, it's far too small for anything else. O'Neill's develop much larger properties.

'So he'd want to live here?' Laura tried to sound nonchalant. 'Rather a big place for one person, as Lady Melling has found out.'

'Oh, Jack intends it to be a family home,' Fiona purred. 'I think you know what I mean, Miss Fenton.'

She looked exactly like a cat who'd stolen the whole bowl of cream.

'Perfectly!'

Laura breathed in deeply. That was why Jack was handling it all himself. He was going to live here. She had suspected that there were probably women in his life, and, for some unknown reason, that idea had been disconcerting. But the thought of Jack O'Neill and Fiona Wilcox setting up home at Selby together made her feel quite sick.

Laura took a call later that morning. The voice was brisk and efficient.

'May I speak to Miss Fenton?'

'Speaking.'

'Hello. This is Jack O'Neill's secretary. He's received your application form and would like you to come in for a chat if possible.'

Laura's heart lurched. That stupid form!

64

Why had India posted it?

'When?' she asked, hoping her voice sounded normal.

'When are you free?'

'This afternoon?'

She wanted to get the farce over as soon as possible. She didn't expect it would be convenient, considering that Jack O'Neill's head office was in London and she was one hundred and fifty miles away and that, as Managing Director, like most of that breed, was likely to have a full diary.

However, she was in for a surprise!

'Excellent!' the voice said. 'Are you able to get into Hereford for three?'

Laura had expected the woman to say Birmingham at least.

'The Chesney Hotel, Wellington Suite.'

Of course, that was where he was staying with Fiona Wilcox.

'Yes, I can,' Laura replied without much eagerness.

'Do you need directions? I can fax them to you.'

'No, I know the Chesney,' Laura replied icily.

'Wonderful!' the woman replied. 'Thank you. We'll see you then.'

Laura replaced the receiver and was staring into space when India came up and touched her arm. Her aunt's eyebrows were raised enquiringly.

'Jack O'Neill?'

'Not quite. His secretary. He's received my application form and wants to have a chat with me, this afternoon!'

Laura's sarcastic tone didn't seem to faze her aunt one little bit.

'That means you'll get the job!' India replied enthusiastically, actually smiling in a satisfied way.

'I don't think so,' Laura returned calmly, although her stomach was churning at the unsettling thought of working closely with him. 'I've made up my mind not to accept, even if he offers it to me.'

'Why, Laura? It will be a wonderful opportunity, especially after having to put up with that horrid Nick.'

India looked extremely disappointed.

'Why? Because I think that I'd be exchanging one man problem for another. Jack O'Neill is thoroughly arrogant.'

'But awfully handsome,' India reminded, her eyes sparkling mischievously. 'Well, I suppose you know what you're doing, but I wouldn't say no to being his personal assistant.'

'Then perhaps you should have applied for the job yourself, India,' Laura retorted tartly. 'Oh, I'm sorry. I'm just feeling fragile,' she added hurriedly.

'All I know is that you're letting things get on top of you, which isn't like you, Laura,'

India responded kindly. 'You need a change, and, of course, you'll still be able to keep an eye on Selby.'

'Not if Fiona Wilcox has anything to do with it,' Laura replied grimly. 'She intimated that she and Jack O'Neill were going to live here!'

'Then do something about it,' India added pointedly.

'What can I do?'

'I don't know, but I'm sure you'll think of something. But you can only do it if you take the job!'

'I may not be offered it,' Laura said.

'Don't worry, I'm sure you will.'

As India walked off down the corridor, Laura frowned. Her aunt had been behaving strangely for ages. Just what was she up to?

CHAPTER SEVEN

Laura turned right across the main road and into the drive, which wound its way upwards towards the elegant hotel. Once the Chesney had been a country house very much like Selby, but its fate had been determined when the owner had sold it to a well-known group of hotel developers.

Laura sighed as she approached, glancing occasionally at the flowers which bordered the drive. She couldn't appreciate the beauty of it all because she had too many things on her mind—the Selby sale, her brush with Nick, handing in her notice and the fact that she had applied for a job with one of the most annoying males she'd ever met. As for Fiona Wilcox . . . Laura grimaced. She wasn't sure why she disliked the girl so much but as she neared the hotel, she had a sudden and unwelcome vision of her and Jack O'Neill playing happy families at Selby!

A moment later, the hotel appeared through the trees, its red and grey stone Georgian façade catching the light of the sun. Laura appreciated old buildings so much but, that day, its beauty seemed lost on her. Soon she was backing her car into a parking space next to a lovely flower bed. Pulling down the sun visor, she scrutinised herself in the mirror and made sure that her make-up was fine. She wanted to be at her best when she said no to O'Neill. She was satisfied with the way she looked that morning.

The perfect executive stared back at her— pristine white shirt under precise navy pin-stripe suit, only a hint of gold at the neck in the form of a dainty chain, which was a family heirloom and as tasteful as the tiny gold studs in her ears. Laura flicked the tiniest bit of fluff off her jacket, slipped off her driving shoes and on with her dressy pair. Then she pulled over her leather attaché case and checked everything was present and in order.

The reception area inside the Chesney was sumptuous. Taking a deep breath, she walked over to the reception desk manned by an efficient girl.

'Laura Fenton. I've an appointment with Mr O'Neill.'

The receptionist had evidently been primed. She smiled enthusiastically and picked up the phone. A couple of minutes afterwards, a young woman appeared and introduced herself as one of Jack's team, who was handling the interviews.

'Hello, I'm Trish, one of the O'Neill team.'

'His secretary?'

'No!' She smiled. 'She's upstairs. I'm handling today's interviews.'

A moment later, Laura was following the girl up to the first floor and the Wellington

Suite. All the lower-floor rooms at the Chesney bore military names. Developers loved using names that had links with past owners, and the Chesneys had military ancestors.

Her feet sunk into the plush carpet as she followed the girl down the wide corridor and approached the elegant door with its highly-polished brass plate. A large leather chair with a striped red seat guarded it.

'The Wellington Suite,' the girl indicated.

'Thank you.'

Next moment, Laura was knocking. She'd expected to be answered by his secretary but, to her surprise, Jack O'Neill himself opened the door. He wasn't dressed casually that day, but looked distinguished and sharp in his designer suit. His hair wasn't tousled like it had been in the morning wind, when he'd been hanging off the branch below her on the hillside, and even his dark eyes seemed softer.

'Laura,' he said, 'I've been looking forward to this.'

All of a sudden, she was confused, not so much by him, but by her reaction. She'd had it all straight in her mind, what she'd say and do. She'd be distant, not disdainful, but she'd certainly let him know that she didn't intend to be the assistant to someone who was trying to destroy her inheritance. Instead, she allowed herself to be escorted, not to the chair in front of the handsome, large desk, but to a dainty little corner table in the mullioned bay window, which was set for coffee. On the window-seat lay an expensive-looking briefcase.

'I didn't order any cakes but, if you want them, I'll ring down,' he said.

He couldn't have been more civil. She decided the man was a chameleon who could turn colour to his own advantage. She couldn't let him take her in.

'No cakes, thank you,' she said coolly as she sat down, totally conscious of him standing behind her as he adjusted her chair. 'This is very nice,' she conceded.

After all, she didn't intend to be rude to him, only turn down the job if it was offered. A moment later, he was seated opposite and pushing in the handle of the cafetiere.

'Looks rather strong, I'm afraid,' he said.

Laura was watching his smooth brown hands at the time and hardly noticed what he said.

'Lovely old place, isn't it?' he went on. 'I expect you know it well.'

She glanced at him sharply. He'd probably been checking up on her. Then she relaxed. Of course he had.

'Yes. I held my eighteenth birthday here,' she replied.

'I expect that was some bash,' he said. 'In fact, my dad used to come here a lot. That's

71

why I chose the place.'

'Did he?' She was taken aback.

'He was fond of this part of Herefordshire. Always talked about it.'

His eyes were soft and distant as if he was fond of it, too. How couldn't he be? It was the loveliest part of England. She didn't say anything, knowing he wanted to continue.

He handed her the coffee cup, leaned back and added, 'Of course, I was brought up in the States. Our family had a house in Maine.'

'Really?' She'd been right about the accent then.

'Yes, but Dad came back here frequently for business and such. He wanted to build up O'Neill's in a place he loved. England was everything to him. It was only business that took him away.'

'So you like it here,' she said calmly. 'Miss Wilcox said you did.'

'Fiona?' The soft look was replaced by a keen sharpness. 'What's she been saying then?'

He looked totally relaxed, but Laura could tell he was disconcerted.

'We had a chat yesterday and she told me that you liked Selby and that maybe you wanted it for yourself.'

He put down his cup and smiled wryly.

'Nice idea, but Fiona's full of those. It's one of her only weaknesses.'

Laura restrained herself, knowing that she shouldn't have said what she did, but she really couldn't help doing it. Somewhere inside, a thought that wasn't really worthy of her popped up—he's going to tear you off a strip for that, Fiona!

'She's so efficient I didn't think she had any faults.'

They laughed and the ugly moment was over.

'Now to business,' he said, getting up and fetching his briefcase.

She watched him open it and draw out what was unmistakably her application form. She felt her heart pound ridiculously as he scanned it.

'Impressive,' he said, 'but I think you know that. However, although the idea of having you as my personal assistant is eminently attractive, I'm not sure if it's entirely feasible.'

'Can you tell me why?' she asked immediately, shocked by his comment.

'I'm not sure that you're on my side.'

She lifted her eyebrows and grimaced.

'Pardon?'

'Laura, my PA would have to be my closest ally.'

She found it extremely difficult to concentrate because she was looking at the corners of his mouth which were turning up deliciously. She felt a tiny throb as she imagined him kissing her. She blinked.

'We'd be almost joined at the hip,' he added.

'And you think that would be uncomfortable?' she heard herself saying.

'I think that it would be delightful, but would it be business?'

'I don't know,' she said.

It was the first time she'd ever revealed in an interview that she didn't know something!

'Neither do I, but I'm tempted.'

'What do you mean I wouldn't be on your side?'

'Candidly, you obviously resent my interest in Selby. Doubtless, your aunt has suggested that if you work with me you can keep an eye on things, but . . .'

'But what? Are you suggesting I don't know my own mind?'

'Of course not. I'm being logical. I want Selby and, as far as I can see, you want to keep it.'

Laura was cornered.

'So what am I doing here?'

'Tell me.'

The moment of truth had arrived. Either she was going to offend him or offend herself. It was her choice.

'I didn't want to come. In fact, I'm here under false pretences,' she responded with candour. 'My aunt posted off the form.'

'Lady Melling persuaded you?'

'Not at all.' He made her feel like a petulant child. 'I filled in the form.'

'And?'

74

His expressive eyes were dancing with mirth. Laura didn't like being laughed at and bristled.

'And . . . and . . . I liked the salary you were offering and last night I felt I needed a change.'

'Last night? You mean from Quinton?'

'Not particularly. Just a change. Nick and I have always got on very well. He'll miss me.'

She was not going to tell him why she'd handed in her notice.

'What's wrong in looking for a better outlet for your talents?' A hint of the old arrogance was in his voice. 'Look at your qualifications, your ambitions. It says here that you were in South America. I was, too.'

'Were you?'

'Lovely country, but utterly brutal.'

'Yes,' Laura said quietly, 'and no-one cares. What I saw there made me sick. But, in spite of its faults, it's a fantastic country.'

She was transported back in vivid memory to its colours, its brashness and its cruelty. They sat in silence for several seconds, then he added, 'And you'd like to go back?'

'I'd like to do some good. Is that ridiculous?'

'I have interests out there.'

Her heart sank. She was afraid what they would be. Maybe O'Neill's had the aspirations that other growing companies had—the exploitation of the local peasants.

75

'At present, I'm building a hospital.'

'Are you?' Her surprise was evident.

'Yes, just outside of Belem.'

He sounded extremely enthusiastic and she instantly warmed to him.

'Tell me more,' she said, and he did! Ten minutes later, they were back to the subject of the PA job. 'But this is England,' he finished, 'and my interests here keep the work ticking over there.'

'Which means that . . .'

'I'm always looking for houses like Selby.'

'Oh, well,' she sighed, 'it's all been very interesting but I can see that we've been wasting each other's time. I've a lot to catch up with for Nick.'

'I don't think so,' he said as she went to pick up her briefcase. 'Why don't we talk a bit more over lunch? Perhaps we can come to a compromise. Believe me, it's a tempting proposition to think of us being joined at the hip.'

Jack O'Neill was certainly the most fascinating man she'd ever met and even for the sake of Selby she couldn't deny herself another couple of hours in his company.

'I'd like that,' she said, picking up her briefcase.

'Wonderful.' He glanced at his watch. 'Good, they've probably got our table ready for us by now.'

He stretched out his hand and took her

case. As they walked together towards the door, Laura realised that he'd known all along that she wouldn't be able to resist his invitation. And she knew that she didn't care.

CHAPTER EIGHT

Throughout lunch, Laura learned quite a lot more about Jack O'Neill.

Several times she wondered why on earth she had thought him disagreeable and arrogant, because that day he was at his most charming.

They chatted as if they'd known each other for years, mainly about his future aspirations for his business. In a way, they were very much like hers. She was surprised at how she had misjudged him on their first meeting. He was so enthusiastic when he described his latest plans for the hospital in construction. O'Neill's was evidently pledged to philanthropy in a big way. Jack patronised several South American charities, which had been company policy for years. Evidently his father had travelled extensively in the continent after leaving England and had been moved by the poverty he saw there.

The food at the Chesney was as excellent as it had always been. She'd chosen a scrumptious fillet of fresh salmon bathed in a lime and coriander sauce. He had beef.

'Umm,' she said, later, 'that was delicious. I'm afraid I can't eat any more. Thank you so much.'

'Coffee?'

'Please.'

She sat back, already realising that she didn't want the lunch to end. It had been wonderful to talk to someone who shared her enthusiasm for the South American continent. He'd applauded her championship of the street children and they'd swapped anecdotes.

'So?' he said and she lifted her eyebrows.

'So, you've heard plenty about me and my ambitions. What are yours?'

He leaned forward and she knew he was genuinely interested.

'Well, I'm not aiming to be a tycoon like you but I intend to be much more successful than I am now. I suppose, ultimately, I'd like to end up as a consultant with my own business. People would come to me with their fine art requests and requirements, and I'd advise them.'

'Interesting concept,' he said, 'and you'd do quite well. You have the connections.'

It was the first time that the old uneasy feeling had gripped her.

'You think so?'

'I certainly do. Forgive me for sounding patronising, but with a family background like yours, you'd be in great demand.'

Laura prickled. Was he saying that was why Nick had given her the job at Quinton's? It was a sore point with Laura, that people thought she was hired because of who she was, not what she could do.

'You're an asset to someone like Quinton. You bring in the work.'

'I don't think my background has anything to do with it.'

'Forgive me again but I think you're being naïve. Of course, it does. You've been brought up in places like Selby. You know the people. You're part of it all. I'm not saying you can't do the job, of course. From what I've seen, you're excellent.'

'Thank you,' she replied icily, knowing that the spell had been broken. 'And that's why you don't want to hire me?' she challenged.

'I didn't say I didn't want to take you on,' he retorted, putting down his cup. 'I'm just commenting on the fact that you'd be a prime asset to anyone in business. Actually, I was complimenting you. My requirements might be a little different. I buy up the kinds of places you know about, and you could advise me on their value and their tasteful restoration.'

He was so cool. She realised that he was referring to Selby again.

'Not that I don't have taste, of course.' His eyes twinkled.

She felt the joke was misplaced, part of that arrogance she'd glimpsed before. She was inexplicably disappointed that he didn't seem to mind that he was hurting her feelings. Laura pursed her lips.

'Mr O'Neill . . .'

'Jack, please.'

'You were right earlier. We're probably not suited.'

A tiny expression of regret suddenly crossed his face.

'I'm afraid that your opinion of me isn't quite what I'd envisaged. I didn't net the job with Nick Quinton solely on my family connections! I'm well qualified to do the job I'm doing.'

'Hold on, Laura, I never said you did.' He appeared sincere.

'It sounded like that.'

She stretched out her hand to pick up her handbag, indicating that she was ready to leave but, a second later, to her enormous surprise, his hand was covering hers. She let it lie there.

'If so, I'm very sorry. There's no-one I'd like better to be by my side.'

She blinked at the expression. He was still holding her hand and she didn't want to withdraw it.

'Maybe I wouldn't fit the bill?'

'What do you mean?' she asked, extricating herself.

'I'm something of a rough diamond. I'm no Quinton.'

'I gathered that,' shc replied, thinking that compared with Jack, who spoke frankly, Nick was a smooth operator.

If that was sophistication, Laura knew which she preferred!

'Then why are we at odds? I think you're the ideal person for me, but am I for you?'

'I thought I was the one who was being interviewed,' she retorted with only a hint of a smile.

'But you have to get on with me.'

'I suppose so.'

'Do you think we could have a good working relationship?'

'I'm not sure.'

She realised that her heart wanted to accept the offer that she'd made up her mind to reject, but her head wasn't convinced.

'We could compromise,' he said, his dark eyes holding hers.

'How?'

'Although I need a PA very quickly, I'm willing to wait a little longer. In fact, I think it would be a good idea if you do think carefully about what we discussed. Maybe we could get to know each other a little better first. I'm sure that I'd like you to work for me, but I want you to be convinced you feel the same. How does that suit?'

Her heart was thudding.

'It's very generous, if rather unconventional.'

'I've never been conventional.' He smiled briefly. 'And it's not generous. When I'm offered the best, I usually take it.'

Reading between the lines, she realised that he was confident she'd take up his offer in the end.

'All right,' she said, stretching out her hand. 'I'll think about your offer.'

Seconds later, he was escorting her to the door and out of the hotel. Laura's head was in a whirl when he saw her to the car. As she switched on the ignition, he bent down and spoke through the open window.

'I do want you, you know.' He straightened as she sat, breathless, trying to understand the inference. 'By the way, I'll probably see you later. I'm picking up Fiona. I'll look forward to it.'

It wasn't exactly what Laura wanted to hear. All she could do was nod curtly and drive off.

*   *   *

'Well?' India asked. 'How did it go?'

Laura thought her aunt looked a trifle nervous, rather as if she was afraid that Laura was going to tell her that it hadn't gone well. She hadn't the heart to tease her aunt, although she felt rather uncomfortable owing to the fact that she'd told India that she'd blankly refuse Jack's offer. In her heart, she knew that she was going to say yes.

'OK.'

She considered how Jack had managed to change her mind. She told herself it had been the generous salary, almost twice as much as Nick was paying. But Laura had never been that interested in money. Job satisfaction was what she craved. Then she realised she wasn't being honest, even with herself. The truth was she'd been swept off her feet by him.

'I take it you have the job,' India said dryly.

Laura nodded, a faint smile playing about her lips.

'He offered it to me.'

'And?'

'I'm thinking it over.'

'Well, that's something, I suppose.' India looked relieved, which didn't escape Laura's notice. 'Does it pay what it said on paper?'

'More.'

'More? He must have liked you,' was her aunt's irritating reply.

'Let's say we compromised.'

Laura found that she was enjoying herself by letting nothing slip. India had been so sure she'd get the job, so she wasn't going to have it all her own way.

'We were hesitant at first, but we came to a mutual agreement. I have some time to think before I commit myself.'

India's eyes sparkled. She looked happier than she'd done for ages.

'I can see you're pleased,' Laura added bluntly. 'Why, India?'

'You should take it,' her aunt replied. 'Why? Because I think the post will be right for you. You'll shine and I'm sure he'll be enormously appreciative.'

'You're so funny,' Laura said. 'One would

think you were friends with him. India, he's going to take Selby off you and turn it into apartments!'

'Is that what he said?'

'Not in so many words, but it's what he does.'

'Well, dear, if you work for him, you will make sure he does it properly.'

'That would be quite a challenge, for both of us,' Laura whispered.

'Yes, and he looks as if he enjoys a challenge,' India remarked. 'Good.'

The satisfied tone in her voice annoyed Laura just a little, but she put it down to the fact that India was relieved that Laura would be able to keep an eye on the Selby sale.

'Well, I suppose I have to break the news to Nick that I'm leaving,' Laura said, sighing.

'He'll be over the moon,' India replied sarcastically. 'When will you start with O'Neill's?'

'I might not,' Laura reminded. 'But if I do, as soon as I like.'

When that would be, she wasn't sure. But she knew that Jack O'Neill wouldn't wait for ever. She'd finished with Quinton's and the catalogues listing the Selby contents were now in the public domain. Then she remembered that Nick had mentioned that someone else had shown an interest in Selby. Knowing who it was would be valuable to Jack O'Neill and she didn't intend to let Nick know that she'd been offered a job with Jack. However, even if she did, Jack was a very powerful client and Nick wouldn't want to upset him by behaving foolishly. The commission from the sale would be too good to lose.

Laura didn't like being sneaky, but Nick wouldn't have behaved differently, if the boot had been on the other foot! Sooner or later, he was going to have to tell India the details of the new interest. Indeed, he had a legal obligation to do so. But she'd like to know sooner rather than later. She wouldn't probe, but she intended to winkle it out of him. Besides, she'd done Nick plenty of favours in her time with him, and there was nothing between them. She'd never really liked him at all. The only good thing that had come out of her job was that she'd gained experience.

Laura had convinced herself of the fact when she rang him.

'Look, Nick, I want to be straight with you. As I told you earlier, I'm handing in my notice.'

Her confession was rewarded by a few seconds of silence.

'It's a pity, Laura,' he said, his tone cold. 'We could have done well together. I hope you're not going to regret it.'

'I don't think so,' she replied. 'At least, the major work is taken care of. The catalogues are at the printers and, of course, I'll sort out everything for you before I clear my desk.'

'Thank you.' He didn't beg her to stay. 'May I ask what are your plans?'

'I have some but, at present, I'd rather not discuss them.'

'Very well. In other words, Nick keep your nose out,' he quipped, but there was a sharp coldness in the gibe.

'I am grateful, you know, for what I learned at Quinton's.'

He didn't reciprocate by thanking her.

'But I felt now was the time to move on.'

'Yes, well, I suppose I asked for it with that disastrous proposal of mine,' he retorted.

She wasn't sure how to answer that, so she didn't.

'I hope that this won't influence your aunt's decision to use Quinton's for the sale, no, sorry, the auction!'

Laura started.

'Auction?'

'She hasn't told you then?'

Laura grimaced as Nick continued.

'Lady Melling phoned me up this morning and told me that she wanted to auction Selby, on the day of the sale.'

His tone said it all. He didn't need to add, 'Personally, I think it's madness. She won't get such a good deal as with a private sale, but I'm afraid she's made up her mind.'

Laura was sifting the information. Why had India decided on that? Why hadn't she mentioned it? Laura couldn't understand it.

'Are you still there?' Nick's satisfied tone riled Laura.

'Yes.'

'Good. Well, I suppose we'll have to have a final meeting, so we can wind up business matters.'

'I suppose,' Laura said unenthusiastically, hoping it wasn't going to be traumatic. 'But, before you go, now there's another buyer in the frame as well as O'Neill, maybe an auction wouldn't be a bad thing after all? Has this new buyer a lot to offer? Who is it?'

'I have to tell your aunt first,' Nick replied stuffily.

Laura oughtn't to have been surprised. After all, it was India's business and Laura had given in her notice.

'Anyway, you'll find out soon enough. You needn't worry.'

She could see that he was enjoying sniping at her.

'Nor you really,' Laura replied tartly. 'Quinton's will still get the commission.'

She didn't ask what reserve price had been put on Selby. She'd leave that until she had it out with India. When she put the phone down, her brow was creased in a frown. She'd thought her aunt had been behaving in a really strange way, but this was even stranger. What was the matter with her? If she was so keen on Jack O'Neill having the house, why had she decided on an auction?

88

As Laura was walking across the hall, preparing herself to have it out with her aunt, the library door opened and Fiona Wilcox flounced out.

'I hear congratulations are in order,' she said, but she didn't look very happy.

Of course, Jack had told his girlfriend about wanting to hire Laura! She didn't feel too happy either. The girls regarded each other.

'I haven't made my mind up yet,' Laura replied icily.

'He's not an easy man to work for,' Fiona added pointedly.

'Doubtless I'll find that out for myself,' Laura countered.

'I was very surprised when I heard he'd offered it to you.'

'Why?'

'Well, I don't want to be rude,' Fiona said, her eyes flicking over Laura, 'but his former PA was rather more experienced.'

'Older?' Laura asked sweetly.

She could be insulting, too. She wasn't going to explain herself to Fiona Wilcox. It suddenly occurred to her that, if she took the job, she might be seeing a great deal of her in the future, which wasn't a pleasant idea. Suddenly, she wondered why she hadn't thought of it before. Working with Jack O'Neill would probably bring her into close contact with Fiona Wilcox. Horrors!

'I don't think you should worry about Jack,'

Laura added ironically. 'I'm extremely competent. Besides, I'm pretty sure that he knows his own mind.'

Fiona nodded, then shrugged.

'Could you see that I have some coffee brought in?'

'Of course,' Laura replied, savouring the one-upmanship and remembering that she'd already dropped Fiona in it with Jack earlier on. You need taking down a peg or two, she thought as the girl closed the library door behind her, and I think I might just be the one to do it. It was a satisfying notion.

A moment later, her aunt was looking out of the study and indicating the library in a humorous by-play.

'Yes, coffee for Miss Wilcox again, I'm afraid, India.' Laura grimaced. 'I'll have a word with Mrs Keyes and then I'd like us to have a chat.'

CHAPTER NINE

As they talked, Laura discovered that India didn't want to discuss her plans in detail, which didn't seem fair as, after all, it was Laura who'd been handling the sale for Nick up to now. Even though she didn't work for Quinton's any longer, it was almost like India was shutting her out on purpose.

'I just thought that an auction would be a better idea. It'll give interested parties a chance to bid,' was all that her aunt would say on the subject. She could be as stubborn as Laura when she wanted to be.

'Do you think there will be other buyers then?'

'Oh, yes,' India replied confidently. 'Nick Quinton has already found someone else.'

'Do you know who it is?'

'He says it's a small consortium, Q Holdings.'

Laura frowned. She'd never heard of them.

'They're smaller than O'Neill's. He's going to give me the details later.'

'So they'll probably be outbid?'

'Possibly.'

'Don't you mind, India, that an auction could bring down the price?'

Laura felt it was only right that she should point it out.

'I've set a fair reserve figure.' She didn't name it! 'Price isn't everything, dear. You should know that. I want Selby to go to someone who really wants it. That is what will make me happy.'

Laura shook her head. India probably meant Jack O'Neill. She couldn't think why he'd made such an impression. India continued.

'I've decided that we'll be holding the auction the day of the contents' sale. And I won't be changing my mind again.'

'All on the same day? It's going to be heavy going, India.'

'I realise that, but I'd like to get it over at once. Now you're up to date.'

Laura could see it was no good probing further, so she gave up.

'I'm sorry if you don't like it, Laura, but my mind is quite made up about this. You shouldn't worry. You ought to be concentrating on this lovely new job you've been offered. You're very lucky, you know. I wish I had my time over again. I'd enjoy working with Jack O'Neill.'

'Really, India, you are scandalous!' Laura wagged her finger at her aunt, whose eyes were sparkling. 'By the way, did you ever hear of any Herefordshire O'Neills?'

'It's an Irish name.'

Her aunt lifted her eyebrows.

'I know. It's just that when Jack, Mr O'Neill,

and I were talking this morning he said something about his father being fond of Herefordshire, even though their base was in the States, and that he talked a lot about it. It sounded as if he'd put roots down round here.'

'Then he had very good taste,' India declared. 'And his son has even better, taking on my niece. I'm going to invite that young man over to lunch tomorrow.'

Laura could see that India wasn't going to answer her question about any O'Neills in Herefordshire. The mystery was deepening! She resolved to sound out Mrs Keyes. She and her husband had been around for years. Perhaps she'd heard of O'Neill Senior.

Laura spent the evening of what had proved to be a most surprising day by trying to clear her desk. Even though she'd handed in her notice, it would have been unprofessional to leave things in a mess. People had to be rung and outstanding matters had to be tied up. She concluded that Nick would probably be looking for someone else to take over from her even now. He'd probably use his girlfriend as a stop gap. She also wondered when he was planning to come down. It would certainly have to be soon. The auction was on Friday. She found that she wasn't looking forward to another confrontation.

When she went to bed, she put Nick out of her mind and tried to read a little, but realised that her mind was far from her book and fixed

93

firmly on the possibility of a new position as Jack O'Neill's right-hand woman. From what she had seen, he appeared to have a hands-on approach to his work, which was surprising, given that as Managing Director he had to be a very busy man. He was probably the kind of boss who delegated. She smiled involuntarily as she thought about him.

His behaviour in the wood when they'd first met had made him seem insufferably arrogant. Then she'd been pleasantly surprised by how well they'd got on when he was looking round the house, which had been followed by the less pleasant surprise that he was going out with Fiona Wilcox. Then she'd had that strange interview, lunched with him, which had been good, and talking about their mutual interests had been quite a revelation.

On top of all that, late that afternoon, as he'd promised and as if she hadn't had enough of him, he'd turned up for Fiona, which had given India the chance to ask him to lunch.

'Wonderful. Thank you, Lady Melling. I assume Laura's told you about my offer.' He'd turned to Laura then. 'My secretary can cope a bit longer, but, hopefully, you'll have made up your mind by the time of the auction.'

So he'd been informed already. News travelled fast! He'd smiled at India, who'd reciprocated as if they were the greatest of friends.

Suddenly, a most surprising thought popped

into Laura's head! Could India be trying to get them together? Maybe that was what it was all about. Did she think that Laura and Jack might get together and Selby remain in the family? It was preposterous, but even entertaining the thought made Laura glow. Then, just as suddenly, that pleasurable heat changed to glowering as she remembered how Fiona had flounced out of the library and she had watched him drive his girlfriend away down the drive again.

Laura's mental confusion deepened at getting so many mixed messages. Maybe Jack was the kind of boss who liked things casual, too, like Nick, who'd got the wrong idea and asked her to marry him.

'For goodness' sake, girl,' she said out loud, 'get your head together. You're losing the plot! You've never been a sucker for a handsome face. You want more than that.'

She lay there, her thoughts in turmoil.

This is absurd, Laura thought finally. What am I thinking of? A few days ago I couldn't stand Jack O'Neill! Now I'm thinking of working for him.

She was still thinking about that when she drifted off to sleep, and the first thing she thought of when she woke in the morning was that it was Saturday and Jack O'Neill was coming to lunch!

*   *   *

The kitchen at Selby was a large and cheerful place, the kind of place someone living in a small house might dream about. It was divided into a long rectangle for the cooking area and a larger rectangle area for eating informally. The whole atmosphere that Saturday morning was one of busy anticipation. India was out in the garden picking peas and Laura was detailed to shell them for her.

Although India liked the Blue Dining-Room on formal occasions, the Selby kitchen was where most of the family eating took place. Laura had dressed up that morning and was wearing a pretty, floral-sprigged dress and matching embroidered casual cardigan. Determined to sound out the housekeeper, she perched herself on a stool and proceeded to watch Mrs Keyes making crème brûlée.

'Ummm, that looks lovely!' she said.

'Thank you, Laura.'

Mrs Keyes raised her eyebrows, an OK-out-with-it sign that Laura recognised. When Laura was a little girl she'd been just the same. She'd come into the kitchen, climb up on the stool and get whatever was worrying her off her chest.

'Do you know if any O'Neills ever lived round here?'

Mrs Keyes stopped mixing.

'Have you asked your aunt?'

'Yes. She didn't know them.' Laura

96

corrected the statement. 'At least, she didn't say she did.'

'The name doesn't ring a bell,' Mrs Keyes said quietly, returning to her task as Laura slipped down from the stool. 'Why do you want to know?'

'It doesn't matter. It's nothing important,' she lied. She looked round casually. 'Would you like me to lay the table while I'm waiting for the peas?'

'Please. Your aunt wants the Worcester out, and we're eating in here.'

'OK.'

As Laura started sorting through the china, wondering particularly why India had chosen to entertain Jack in the kitchen, she failed to notice the housekeeper's surreptitious glances in her direction. If she had, she'd have been even more suspicious that both her aunt and Mrs Keyes were hiding something from her.

Laura threw off the apron she was wearing to shell the peas and hurried to answer the door as the shrill sound of the bell filled the air. Jack couldn't have come half an hour early? The lunch was nowhere near ready. To her utter surprise, Nick was standing on the step.

'Good heavens, what are you doing here? It's Saturday.'

'I know,' he said, 'but we have things to discuss, and it's going to be a busy week.'

'Still, it's not like you,' she said, 'giving up

your weekend.'

'Do we have to stand here? May I come in?'

Laura breathed in deeply. She would have loved to have said no, but it wouldn't have been fair. As she showed Nick into the office, she was cursing the fact he'd turned up today of all days! She only hoped that Jack wouldn't show up immediately.

'OK,' she said, indicating a chair and sitting down herself. 'What shall we talk about?'

Nick settled down as if he had all the time in the world.

'I'm sorry, Nick. I don't want to be rude but we have guests for lunch.'

'It won't take long,' he said. 'Besides, I'm really killing two birds with one stone. I'm on my way to see Fiona Wilcox.'

'Why do you want to see her? Couldn't it have waited until Monday?'

'The library has been on to me about some of the books, and we have things to sort out before the sale. You don't have to bother. It's all in hand.'

'I'm not. Look, I've cleared my desk. That pile is . . .'

Laura explained it all very clearly. He must see she'd done more than most people would, who'd just handed in their notice.

'Very efficient. Thank you, Laura,' he said, putting the files together. She could see that he was in a very strange mood. 'Another reason I'm here is that I thought that I ought to tell you more about this new interest in Selby.'

'Does my aunt know?'

'Yes.'

She couldn't understand why India hadn't told her. A surreptitious glance at her watch confirmed that Jack's arrival was imminent.

'But I want you to know as well.'

She felt really frazzled, almost panicky. Her nerves were totally on edge. In a moment, she might have to reveal who she was contemplating working for. On the other hand, she wanted to know whatever he was ready to tell her. She kept imagining she could hear the car coming up the drive!

'You're really on edge, Laura. Who's coming? Royalty?'

'Don't be ridiculous,' she snapped, getting up and opening the door. He took the hint and rose as well.

'I think we should save the post mortem for Monday, don't you?'

She watched him pick up the files. This time, she really could hear the car approaching! Nick followed her into the hall. He was still hovering.

'It's important that you know!' he emphasised. 'I promise I'll make it quick,' he added.

'Hurry up then. Please.'

She opened the door, darting a look outside. Thankfully, Jack hadn't made it yet.

Next moment, to her utter horror, Nick had plumped down the files on the step and had his arms around her.

'What are you doing?' she squeaked.

'What I want to do most of all.'

'Let me go!' He took no notice and he was holding her very tightly.

'Q Holdings is me, Laura. I'm in the bidding for Selby. I intend to own this place with my partners.'

'What?'

She stopped struggling and stared at him with shocked eyes. His were pleading.

'I want you to reconsider my offer, to marry me, to be part of it, too. Please? Believe me, Q Holdings stands a very good chance of winning!'

'You are Q Holdings,' she repeated.

'Yes. I've declared my interest now. It's all legal. Will you please listen to what I'm saying! I want you. I need you. You'll come round to it in the end. We'll make a wonderful team.'

The Mercedes came to a crunching halt on the gravel drive and Laura realised to her horror that she was still in Nick's arms. She disengaged herself slowly and as with as much dignity as she could muster.

'I want you to go now, Nick,' she hissed. 'We'll discuss this on Monday! I don't think we have anything else to say.'

He shrugged and glanced over towards the waiting car.

'I think Prince Charming has arrived,' he said sarcastically. 'Well! Feet under the table early, eh?'

He looked grim. As he walked over to the car nonchalantly, the window slid down. Jack looked even grimmer!

'Afternoon, O'Neill. Nice to see you again. Have a good lunch.'

His artificial jauntiness was rewarded by a curt nod. A moment later, a mortified Laura was watching Nick get into his car, and Jack approaching. As he strode over to her, she knew that her cheeks were blazing, because they felt incredibly hot. His face was set.

'Hello,' she said, swallowing, her mouth very dry.

'How are you?' he asked, his tone harsh.

'Absolutely fine.' She had never felt worse. She glanced at her watch. 'Bang on time!' she said. 'Lunch is almost ready.'

As they crossed the hall towards the drawing-room where India was waiting, he said quietly, 'You told me that you got on with Quinton. Now I know how well.'

CHAPTER TEN

If it hadn't been for the earlier fiasco with Nick, everything would not have been perfect, but better. However, it had happened and Laura couldn't get it out of her head that Jack had seen the two of them in a close embrace. It was a most awkward situation.

Laura told herself time and again during lunch that the episode with Nick was exactly the kind of thing that Jack had mentioned at the interview, when he'd felt suspicious about her application and he'd said that he wanted her on his side. She decided that after what he'd seen, he would be ever more suspicious. After all, she'd appeared to be consorting with the enemy! Did he also know that Nick was part of the rival Q Holdings consortium? Her old boss had said he'd already declared his interest.

Nick's pig-headedness had cast a blight on the growing relationship between her and her new employer. She would have to have it out with Jack, but what could she say without seeming ridiculous?

As she tried to relax and listen to the animated conversation India was holding with him, she considered what the word relationship meant in that context. She told herself hurriedly that what she was really worrying about was that the incident with Nick might have jeopardised their working relationship in the future.

'A penny for them, Laura,' India quipped. Laura smiled self-consciously. Jack was regarding her quizzically, too.

'Sorry? What?'

'We're talking about the sale, dear!'

The slight raising of India's eyebrows reminded Laura that she should have been paying attention. Her aunt was evidently sounding Jack out!

'What particular changes could you see being made here, Jack,' she went on, 'without losing the character of the old place? I mean for example, if this were one of your new apartments, would you retain the features? That rose up there in the ceiling dates back to the eighteenth century, as does the cornice. I've spent so many happy hours in here. Do you know we always held the dances in this kitchen. Sounds bizarre, but it was quite different before. It used to be two huge rooms, the Blue Dining Room was the other, but my father had it partitioned off when he put in this kitchen. It was a wonderful room when I was a teenager!'

India's eyes sparkled at the memory.

'I'm sure it was,' Jack said. 'And it still has very fine features. I agree with you about the rose, Lady Melling. The cornice is magnificent.'

Jack raised his eyes, considering it. Then he frowned and narrowed his eyes at Laura, who realised she was frowning, too, because she was at a loss to understand how India could bring herself even to talk about what was going to happen to Selby when she was gone! The whole thing was too raw for Laura to contemplate.

'I thought maybe Laura might have told you that O'Neill's is not in business to destroy the character of superb old houses,' he added. 'It was quite an important point yesterday, wasn't it, Laura?'

She found herself bristling at the reproof. He had such power to annoy, and cajole! She looked hard at him and he responded with a keen glance.

'I personally ensure that our restorations are tasteful and in keeping with the character of the places I buy.'

'If they were not,' India responded, 'then I can assure you that I wouldn't be feeling as relaxed as I do now about it.'

'I'm glad of that,' Jack said. 'And I'm very grateful. Also I find it extremely interesting to hear what the place was like in the old days.'

'Thank you, Jack,' India said, smiling and leaning back. 'I guarantee you would have loved it then. Would you like more lamb? There's heaps.'

'Please.'

'It's ages since I've entertained. I like to see

a young man with a good appetite!'

Jack seemed to relax more as the meal continued, while Laura felt herself tensing up, although she was doing her best for India's sake. But her nerves felt like tight strings, especially when she and Jack brushed against each other as she leaned forward to pick up her wine glass. She knew he'd noticed, too, by the look in his eyes.

Laura looked away quickly as Mrs Keyes popped in to clear away the second course.

'Now, who's for this lovely crème brûlée?' India asked briskly. 'It's my housekeeper's speciality.'

'I certainly am,' Jack declared, offering his dish.

Later, coffee arrived in the Georgian silver set, and was whisked away, too. Laura felt uncomfortably full and yearned for fresh air.

'Why don't you and Jack take a turn in the garden?' India asked, who must have been reading her mind. 'I'm sure you have lots to talk about.'

She got up and Jack rose. A moment later, he was turning to Laura.

'Yes. Why don't we? You can fill me in on anything I missed before.'

The inference was obvious. He was a master of innuendo.

'Thanks for the wonderful meal, Lady Melling.'

'No, thank Mrs Keyes. She's a splendid

cook,' India declared. 'Don't go too far. I'll expect you both back at three-thirty for tea in the drawing-room.'

'Phew!' Jack said, smiling at Laura.

After a leisurely walk, they finally stood together in the White Rose Garden, which had been planted by a Melling ancestor over two hundred years ago. The perfume of the blossoms filled the air on the most perfect of summer afternoons.

'Heavenly,' Laura said, almost to herself.

Adjusting her sunglasses, she walked over to a quaint little seat in the arbour. He followed and she realised that she was even conscious of his feet as they crunched on the gravel. She could feel his energy in the atmosphere, setting her emotions on fire. They sat down together and still didn't speak. They'd chatted about trivialities as they'd crossed the lawns and walked through the walled garden and on into the farthest parts of the estate.

She'd remarked on the amount of butterflies that were around and he'd asked her the names of one or two of the more obscure plants. They'd leaned on the fence and looked across at the distant shapes of the hills, but now, ensconced in that little arbour and out of sight of the house in what seemed like their own little world, Laura found her senses reeling.

'I love this place,' she said.

'The atmosphere hasn't escaped me either,'

106

he said.

'What do you feel?' she asked.

'Why do women always want to know how a man feels?' was the surprising reply and she cursed herself inwardly for being disappointed. 'I suppose . . . because, to us, feelings are the most important thing,' she retorted. 'Why did you mention the atmosphere then?'

She could see that soon they'd be at loggerheads again.

'It's warm out here. It's beautiful.' She could see he was struggling. 'The roses are great, but they're all white.'

'It's a white garden.'

'I've seen another of those, at Sissinghurst. It was impressive.'

'But that wasn't one of your acquisitions,' she teased.

'No, even I can't run to that!' he said wryly. 'And I haven't acquired Selby yet. I have a rival, and, of course, there may be others now the house is to be auctioned. By the way, I've started my own inquiries about Q Holdings, and Nick's financial position. Are you going to tell him about my investigations?'

'Why should I? I don't work for him any more.'

He took off his glasses, squinted into the sun and rubbed his eyes as if he was exhausted. It was the first indication of ordinary weakness that she'd seen in him. Of course, he must be tired, given his enthusiasm for work. She softened.

'But you're still in contact,' he added and her sympathetic moment dissolved quickly.

'Yes.'

She stiffened. Now was the time to declare there was nothing between her and Nick, but she didn't, because she wasn't sure if Jack was interested in her or only in business. She knew then that she wanted a proper sign, which wasn't forthcoming.

'I have to be, over the sale. But I am on your side.' She was trying.

'I'm glad,' he said, not moving. 'But I sense that all this is very difficult for you.'

'It's difficult because . . .' She found she couldn't frame the words.

'Because this is your home and, not only do I want to buy it, he does, too.'

She nodded. He put his glasses on again.

'You shouldn't worry,' he said. 'It'll be safe in either case. But, of course, I believe that my interest is more important than his.'

'Naturally,' she said, biting back. 'Business is always the most important. My father taught me that.'

He had certainly known how to subordinate his personal life! The old bitterness was still there, she realised. He'd never spent any time with any of them really. He'd wanted to, but he never did. And, now he never would.

'As for my brother, he's wandering in Nepal while this goes on. Men!'

108

To her horror, she felt tears starting in her eyes, but he couldn't see them. He didn't speak for a while. Then he put a hand on her arm. It felt like she was burning.

'I'm sorry.' He shook his head. 'You should learn to trust, Laura. If you are to work for me, you'll have to.' He stood up. 'This has been very pleasant.'

He offered his hand. She took it and she could almost feel the pulse in hers beating. Her heart was shrieking at him to say something meaningful.

'I look forward to working with you. And I'm glad you're on my side. Let's hope it stays that way.'

'Believe me, I don't mix business with personal matters.'

She withdrew her hand. It was the best thing she could think of to explain what had happened between her and Nick.

'I understand,' he said, 'and you'll find out I don't either. Seeing that the auction is on Friday, how about starting for me on Monday? By then the thing will be settled, one way or another. But feel free to call me any time, if you need to. Now, shall we walk back to the house?' He glanced at his watch. 'If we go the long way round, we'll just be in time for tea.'

*   *   *

'I've really enjoyed today,' India declared

happily as she waved Jack off down the drive. She'd been sparkling all through tea. 'How about you?'

'I've mixed feelings,' Laura replied truthfully.

'I don't believe that you don't find him charming. So what's the matter?'

'I think I should ask you that!' Laura blurted out. 'You were all over him! Oh, I'm sorry. That was terribly rude. I didn't mean it.'

All the light had gone out of India's face. She looked both hurt and puzzled. Laura loathed herself for being so petty.

'I'm just . . .' She shook her head hopelessly.

'Come on, Laura,' India said, shaking off her shock. 'Don't worry. You haven't offended me. Come on now.'

'India, I'm so sorry. That was unforgivable.'

'No, I'm the one who should apologise for my behaviour. I admit I got a little carried away. Entertaining Jack O'Neill made me feel a little less old. I'm a silly old woman.'

'But you're not, India. You're marvellous! I hope I'm like you when I'm sixty!' Laura said in utter sincerity.

'It's nice of you to say so, Laura, but I have no illusions. You see, dear, Jack reminds me of someone I used to know, someone I was very fond of.'

Her voice was sad and, in the dim light of the hall, India's figure suddenly seemed to stoop, making her appearance quite different

110

from the energetic person she'd been an hour ago. Laura had never seen India looking like that and wondered what was coming next. Her father had always hinted at the fact there was a good reason why India had never married. There had been someone, but Laura had never been able to find out who it was. This was the first time that India had ever mentioned it.

'Come on, India,' she said cheerfully, although she didn't feel it. 'Let's go into the snug. You look worn out.'

India sat down in her favourite chair and Laura drew the curtains to stop the late afternoon sun blinding them. A faint wind stirred the drapes, cooling down the stuffy room. Then India was talking again!

'He was charming, too, volatile, interesting. You'd have loved him, Laura. Having that young man in the house suddenly made him come alive for me again.'

Laura didn't know what to say. She couldn't pry. She was only sorry that she'd shouted at her aunt. She knew that, if she ever heard it, India's love story wouldn't have a happy ending.

'I'm selfish,' Laura declared, sitting down on the floor at India's feet and staring at the carpet. 'Please don't worry. I'm glad you invited Jack. I'm just all wound up, and I don't like it.'

'You're not selfish, you know. In fact, you're

a great comfort to me. You always have been. I think I understand what's the matter. You like him, don't you? But you're not sure if you can trust him.'

'How do you know that, India?'

'Let's say I'm a lot older than you, dear. I may be an old maid, but I do have some experience.'

The unknown love again, Laura thought.

'I don't want to think I don't trust him, but I still have difficulty imagining him . . .' Laura looked down at the carpet.

'Living in this house?'

'Yes.'

'And?'

'And nothing.'

'Living here with Fiona Wilcox?'

'Don't!' Laura shuddered. The room felt so close she could hardly breathe. She moved irritably. 'Oh, I don't know what's the matter with me!'

'It's known as jealousy.' India's voice was soft.

'How can it be? Jack O'Neill and I have hardly said two words to each other.'

'My dear, if you want something, you have to go for it. Personally I think that Jack might be the right man for you.'

'For goodness' sake,' Laura said, getting up, shocked by India's last remark. 'I can't believe you're matchmaking. Jack might be handsome and charming but, remember, he's going to take Selby off us.'

'Well, not if he was with you,' India replied pointedly.

'Please, India, don't. Is that what this is all about, why you asked him to lunch, why you appear to like him so much?'

'Perhaps!' her aunt answered candidly. 'You can't blame me for that. I'd like to see you and Jack O'Neill get closer. Although you didn't hit it off in the beginning, in my opinion, he seems the right kind of young man for you!'

Laura stared at her aunt, who, she could see, really meant what she said.

'India, please, I'm not for sale, too!'

Laura's face crumpled. India jumped up from her chair too quickly and half stumbled. Laura caught her! Her aunt's face was full of apology as she righted herself.

'I'm sorry, Laura, if I've upset you. I shouldn't have even thought it might work.'

'It's all right,' Laura said miserably. 'We're as bad as each other. We keep saying the wrong things. You know how I hate all this. It's impossible! In any case, someone else besides Jack might bid for Selby, and win!'

She waited to see what India would make of that.

'Over my dead body!' India retorted, coming back to herself. 'I don't want that lounge lizard buying my house!'

'You mean Q Holdings? That Nick Quinton? You should never have taken that position

113

with him.'

India grimaced, then nodded. Laura wondered when Nick had told her? Laura frowned. Her aunt had clearly not thought things out. Whatever would she say if she knew that Nick was the one who wanted Laura and had dangled the idea in front of her that, if she relented, she'd be able to keep Selby in the family?

'Even if Nick or Jack don't get it, someone else will. Anyway, when did he tell you about Q Holdings?'

'Yesterday,' India said.

'You mean you knew that Nick was a rival bidder?' Laura considered the revelation. 'That's why you invited Jack to lunch?'

'I'm afraid so,' India confessed.

'I wish you'd told me, India! That's almost sharp practice. If it comes to light that you favoured Jack . . .'

Laura recalled the look on Nick's face when Jack arrived and what he'd said—feet under the table. She knew Nick too well. He would take anything as far as he could, to get what he wanted.

'India, it wasn't a good move. What Nick is doing is perfectly legal. Although he's been handling the sale, he has declared his interest in Selby, which gives him the right to bid for it.'

'Oh, dear, I wasn't thinking,' her aunt said.

Laura pursed her lips. It was not like India,

who was extremely astute in business matters. 'Should I ask him to lunch as well?'

Laura couldn't decide whether India was serious or not, but she shook her head anyway. 'No,' she said decidedly. 'At least you've changed to an auction which might limit the damage.'

'It is my house after all!' India said sadly.

'For now, India.'

It would have been cruel to twist the knife. Laura had known that, in the end, India was bound to regret selling the Hall. But it was her property, not Laura's, whose business brain began to quickly calculate the options. Maybe Nick had been guilty of an unfair advantage, too. Perhaps he was meeting Fiona Wilcox to winkle out information as to Jack's intentions, but Laura decided the girl wouldn't say anything out of place because she wanted Jack to buy Selby.

In any case, Nick knew everything about Jack's finances as O'Neill's had been in the hunt before he was. India's expression was still worried as Laura walked over to the window and stared out, thinking it was all such a mess! For the umpteenth time that day she remembered Jack's set expression as he got out of the car after he'd seen her and Nick together. Perhaps he really thought they were an item. Maybe he truly suspected she was a spy.

CHAPTER ELEVEN

The viewing days were extremely busy. A variety of people, both public and trade, arrived to look over Selby and its contents. The catalogues had been sold out and had raised quite a sum at five pounds a copy.

Nick had drafted in a couple of PR people from an agency as well as a local auctioneering firm. Laura ought to have been pleased to see such a good turn-out but, as Friday approached, she was getting more and more depressed. It was like watching one's life slipping away. She had so many happy memories of the place, which was soon to be just a memory!

She flitted about aimlessly watching the public and dealers alike looking over the Selby treasures. She had been forced to answer several questions as to why the library wasn't accessible, although the catalogue had an adequate picture, and had explained that the contents were not in the sale owing to the fact that the British Library was buying the collection.

Laura thought bitterly about Fiona, ensconced in splendid isolation, sipping coffee and, doubtless, thinking of future glory! India had withdrawn to her bedroom, which was also out of bounds. She'd said that she wasn't in the least upset, but Laura knew she was and had begged her to go and stay with her friend, Betty, in Hereford, for the last couple of days. Naturally, India had declined.

Jack had not put in an appearance, but she hadn't expected him to really. He was definitely distancing himself from her. Laura had also been keeping out of Nick's way. He seemed to be popping up everywhere, but she couldn't blame him for that, she supposed. She'd ducked into the snug to avoid him walking grandly down the stairs as if he owned the place. He'd had a smug smile on his face, which boded no good. A moment later, Laura's intuition told her something was in the air! India was standing at the top of the staircase, beckoning frantically.

Laura followed her aunt into her bedroom, which was not its usual, immaculate self. A stack of boxes was waiting by the door for collection. India had been forced to have a clear-out over the last few weeks.

India sighed, shook her head, then sat down on the padded stool in front of the mirror and indicated that Laura should sit on the bed.

'I've just had a visitor, Nick Quinton, to inform me that Jack O'Neill has pulled out of thc salc!'

Laura's heart leaped. Jack had given up! She couldn't believe it, but a cold feeling was creeping over her and her hands felt clammy. India continued in a voice, which had just a hint of a tremble.

'I had the satisfaction of telling him that I knew already because Jack had phoned me himself ten minutes before that lounge lizard appeared. I've been shaking all over ever since!'

'But Jack can't have. He was so keen. He told me so,' Laura said. 'I can't believe he's pulled out. I've seen his secretary downstairs.'

Laura sounded frantic but, inside, she was icy calm, because she suddenly knew it was something to do with her. India put a hand up to her cheek and brushed away a tear. Laura ran over to her aunt.

'Come on, India, what did he say? Don't worry, please.'

'He was very polite, in fact, the perfect gentleman.'

India's lip was quivering and Laura was so wrapped up in the drama of the situation that she didn't think it strange that India could be so upset when there was still every possibility of a successful sale to someone other than Nick. Laura couldn't think of anything else to do except put her arm round India's shoulders. India looked up at her and sniffed.

'I understand how upset you are, but not the reason entirely. You will find a buyer and if you don't want the place to go to Nick, then you must withdraw!' Laura pleaded.

'I wanted Jack O'Neill to buy Selby, that's all,' India said stubbornly.

'None of this is making sense, India. Please explain to me. What did he say? If you don't tell me, I'll ring him myself.'

'No, Laura. He said he was pulling out for personal reasons, that his interest in Selby has changed. He said that he believed that Q Holdings would do a good job with the place and that I oughtn't to worry. He'd checked them out and they were financially sound. He also said that you would still be around anyway to keep an eye on things.'

Laura felt absolutely numb. She had no idea what he meant, but it sounded as if her job with him was a non-starter. India was looking at her steadily and she felt more than uncomfortable.

'I don't want to ask you this, Laura, but have you any idea why Jack pulled out? Has something happened that you haven't told me?'

It was the moment of truth. Laura breathed in, then nodded.

'All right. This may have no bearing on anything, India, but one of the things I didn't tell you was that Nick Quinton asked me to marry him.'

'What?'

'I'm afraid so. It was when he came down a week ago. I didn't know then that he was interested in Selby. I was flabbergasted when he suggested we should get together and make a go of it. He wanted us to live here together

119

and he even added you could live here, too! It was almost an ultimatum. I couldn't tell you, could I? It wasn't really appropriate.'

'You turned him down, and he went after Selby anyway?'

'Yes. I wouldn't even contemplate living with him, never mind marrying him. But the second thing I didn't tell you was that the day that you invited Jack to lunch, Nick turned up unexpectedly. You were preparing the drinks in the drawing-room, I think. He told me about Q Holdings. You should have told me he'd contacted you the day before, India! I would have been prepared then. Well, he proposed again, grabbed hold of me and Jack turned up at that very moment, when I was struggling to get away. I expect he thought we . . .' She shrugged.

'He didn't like it,' India said.

'No, he didn't, although I can't for the life of me imagine why. There's absolutely nothing between us. He's never said anything that made me feel he was interested in me. This is ridiculous, India! The man wouldn't pull out of a lucrative business deal for some silly whim. It's not as if we were married or something! I don't understand men!'

'I never have,' India said. 'That's why I'm still single. I'm glad you told me, Laura.'

'Why? It will make no difference. I'm so sorry, India, if Jack pulling out has been anything to do with me. It sounds like

120

arrogance to even assume it has, and I've said I'll work for the man.'

Laura suddenly felt anger as well as disappointment. Jack evidently wasn't the man she thought. India had started to powder her nose.

'It's all right, dear, I'm feeling better now. It's been a shock, but I'll get over it. I wonder if Jack O'Neill had asked you to marry him, if you'd have given him the same answer.'

'Not again, please, India. He didn't, nor is he likely to, given that he's fixed up with Fiona Wilcox and . . .' Laura didn't finish the sentence.

'But if he had?'

'I honestly don't know.' The thought was delectable.

'You wouldn't turn him down flat?'

Laura smiled.

'What do you think?'

'The same as you, I expect,' India returned. 'I've been thinking about what you said a few days ago, that I should go and visit Betty while all this is going on. I think I will after all. I want to get away from that mob downstairs, to prepare myself for tomorrow.'

'I think that's a very good idea,' Laura said. 'Shall I ring her?'

'No, dear, I will. Why don't you run down to Mrs Keyes and ask her to make you a cup of tea, or something stronger even? You look as though you need it.'

'Don't you?'

'No,' India said decidedly. 'The fickleness of the opposite sex never ceases to amaze me. I shall never understand them if I live to be one hundred.'

'You will, India,' Laura said quietly. 'You're stronger than you know. When will you be back?'

India consulted her watch.

'I'm not sure. Before it's dark, anyway. It'll give this lot time to go, and don't worry about me.'

As Laura closed the bedroom door behind her, she knew that she was not only going to worry about India, but herself as well. If Q Holdings was financially sound, then it was very likely that they would triumph over all comers and Nick would have Selby. As she paused on the stairs and looked down into the hall, which was still full of people poking about and exclaiming over their personal effects, she was deciding that, at least, Fiona Wilcox wouldn't be mistress of Selby, which was a cold kind of comfort.

Then, suddenly, to her chagrin, Nick was standing at the bottom of the staircase and there was no chance of avoiding him.

'Hi,' he said. 'I assume you've been talking to India.'

'I have. I don't want to discuss it, Nick.'

'You're going to have to, you know.'

'Why am I?' She rounded on him. 'Can you

122

imagine how I feel?'

'Because O'Neill has pulled out?' His eyes were shifty. 'You still have my support, and you could still have Selby, you know. We were always a good team. It's not too late.'

'I don't think so,' she hissed coldly. 'I need some fresh air.'

Once she was standing out in the air, looking across the cars parked all along the drive in the direction of the White Garden, she felt anger bubbling up again, which matched the look of the sky. She could see they were in for a storm! She felt like giving Jack a piece of her mind. He'd betrayed her. Did she want to work for someone like that? Surely, as his prospective personal assistant, it might have been polite to have let her know what was happening. He'd said she should ring whenever she liked.

When Laura made a decision, she carried it out. She was perfectly aware that this might be the end of a business relationship with Jack O'Neill even before it had begun. She dialled Jack's number and, putting the tiny phone to her ear, walked over to the shrubbery, where the garages backed on to the house, scuffing the gravel with her foot impatiently as she went. India's car was parked outside, so she hadn't gone yet.

Jack had a lovely voice on the phone, mellow, but measured and, although she didn't notice it in her frame of mind, carrying a rather sad tone.

'Laura, how are you?'

Tears were stinging behind her eyes.

'I don't know how you can ask that. You pulled out of the sale!'

'Yes.'

'And you never thought of telling me?'

'I let your aunt know as soon as I made the decision.'

'And you think that was enough?' Laura asked grimly.

'I don't get you.'

'You could have explained.'

'Look, Laura, when you get to know me, you'll realise that every decision I make is a considered one. This one was in Selby's best interest, and yours and your aunt's.'

'You think so?' The bitterness was welling up. 'You realise that Q Holdings will get the place.'

'Isn't that the general idea?'

'I don't understand,' Laura said slowly. 'You think that we want them?'

'It's quite clear to me that you do.'

'How do you make that out?'

'Laura, I don't want to discuss my decision.'

'How do you think we could ever work together, if you can't give me a simple answer to a simple question?'

Her temper was flaring. If he'd just tell her that was the reason, she'd tell him there was nothing between her and Nick.

'Let's say then that if I bought Selby I'd be interested in everything that goes with it, and that's hardly likely now, is it? I like to win, Laura! I have to go now. I have another call coming in. Ring me later if you like.'

'I think we've said it all, Jack,' she snapped.

'Goodbye!'

A moment later, she was running for the side door of the house as the storm broke. She met India inside, making her way down the corridor to the back entrance.

'You're not going in this surely! Wait until it's over,' Laura advised.

'Sorry, dear, but I've just phoned Betty. She wants to meet me in Hereford for tea. Don't worry. I'll be fine dashing over to the garage.'

She was pulling her coat around her and opening her umbrella. Laura sighed and stood aside as India dashed out of the door. She looked at her mobile. Should she ring Jack again, have it out with him?

'Oh, what's the use?' she said out loud. 'I can't explain and he can't, either or won't! What basis is that for any kind of relationship?'

* * *

Jack O'Neill stood looking out of the window of the Wellington Suite. He felt extremely miserable, even cheated, which made him irritable. He'd agreed to see her, but he wasn't

125

sure why. As he'd told Laura, he liked to win, and it appeared this time he'd backed a loser.

He was out of sorts anyway. The blazing row he'd had with Fiona the evening before had been the last straw. He would never understand women. Then the phone on the desk rang. It was Reception.

'Yes? Show her up. And bring the tea in about fifteen minutes, please.'

Jack sighed, then picking up the Selby catalogue, he sat down on the big leather chair by the fireplace, stretched out his long legs and started to leaf through it idly as he waited for his visitor.

CHAPTER TWELVE

The moment Laura had been dreading for the last six months had finally arrived. She would have liked not to be present at the auction, but she had no option. She and India were sitting together, half-hidden behind a curtain as the bidding commenced.

The local auctioneer was a cheery chap, but Laura failed to be amused at his breezy manner. The house was to go first, he'd said. As Nick was a bidder, he'd had to hand over the job to a neutral party. They'd had no other declarations of interest, but as Laura looked round, she was hoping.

The ballroom was full to capacity, packed with unknown, potential buyers. It would only take one! Her glance kept returning to the man seated at the back. Every time he looked over at her, she looked away. She hadn't phoned him again and she'd been surprised to see him arrive. Even though she almost hated him, he looked impressive in his sharp business suit. He'd make a striking figure anywhere. Suddenly, he caught her glance and held it. He had the effrontery to smile at her. She breathed in deeply and looked away. She had a letter in her bag which she intended to hand over—her resignation, for the job that never was! She felt entirely miserable, but, surprisingly enough, India looked quite cheerful. She was a tough old bird!

'I never imagined there would be so many people,' her aunt said quietly, patting her arm. 'I see Mr O'Neill made it.'

'He's got a nerve,' retorted Laura.

'He certainly has,' India agreed, but she didn't seem too upset about it.

'I don't know how you can be so calm about it, India. I wouldn't be here if it wasn't for you.'

'I know, dear. I'm sure everything will come out all right in the end.'

Laura almost felt hostile to India, who'd been everything to her over the last twenty years! She had to sit back, grin and bear it, watching her inheritance go down the drain. Then she felt remorse. She wasn't being fair. It was her aunt's decision. She could do what she liked with her money.

Besides, India had told Laura she'd made her will in favour of Laura and her brother, Sam, and, of course, Laura had had her pick of any personal things she wanted. So if Selby had to go, then it was best it went to someone who'd pay most for it. She wondered if a pop star or a footballer might buy it, anyone but Nick, she prayed, determined to be calm.

Her ex-boss was sitting in the front, looking confident, while her boss-that-never-was kept fidgeting in his seat. Why had he come? Laura deliberately took her eyes off him and fixed them on the auctioneer, who was getting underway. It was a bit like waiting for the execution!

She remembered afterwards how quickly the house went. Three bidders evolved. One of them was Nick, another was represented at the back of the room and one was bidding on the telephone. Q Holdings was forced to pull out as the price rose rapidly. Laura could feel India gasp and, involuntarily, they sought each other's hands and clasped them.

The mystery company on the telephone eventually won the bidding. During the murmur that followed and the settling down for the beginning of the effects, Nick turned and caught Laura's eye, then got up and stormed out. He looked furious. She felt able to look across to where Jack was then, but his seat was empty. He probably couldn't stand the disappointment either, she thought. Well, it's all over. I suppose they'll tell us soon who's got it.

Then she saw him. He'd taken over the seat Nick had vacated and was keenly observing the proceedings. He didn't even have the grace to look her way, but, ten minutes later, Laura was totally nonplussed. Why, if he didn't want the house, was he bidding for the effects? Did he want to hurt her? India kept patting her on the arm as he bought one thing after another. Totally exhausted, Laura watched the auctioneer's clerk show the portrait of India.

Well, at least, Jack wasn't going to get that!

Laura started to bid against him but when the price became ridiculous, she conceded. For the first time since the start of the effects' sale, he looked her way with triumph in his eyes. All Laura's pent-up disappointment suddenly hit her and she got up from her seat.

'Where are you going?' India asked calmly.

'Out of here! I can't bear it any longer.'

'Laura,' India said, looking up at her, 'I'm sorry I put you through all this.'

'Just don't say any more, please.'

I am not going to cry she told herself firmly as she hurried out of the ballroom as bidding began again. A moment later, she was rushing upstairs, making for where she belonged. She ran through the Picture Gallery, now empty of all the portraits of all her ancestors who'd managed to keep Selby safe for hundreds of years, towards the Boudoir, her grandmother's old sitting-room, her favourite place in the house.

Inside, even that had changed. Someone had moved the old tester bed in there, but they hadn't touched the harp, which stood beside it. It was Lot Number 269 in the catalogue, so why hadn't it been taken downstairs? She began to cry silently, as she went over to it and ran a finger over its strings. It had been cleaned up carefully for the sale, and emitted a plaintive cascade of notes. She sat on the bed and sobbed. A moment later, she told herself not to be such a sentimental fool and scrubbed her eyes with her handkerchief. Suddenly, she was conscious that someone was standing in the doorway.

'What are you doing here?' she sniffed.

'The same as you, escaping from downstairs.'

'I don't know what you mean,' she said.

A moment later, Jack was sitting on the bed beside her, his dark eyes full of sympathy.

'How did you know I was here? What do you want?'

'I have what I want,' he said, 'almost.'

She frowned and sniffed again. She should have been angry with him, but she wasn't. All she felt was empty. She shook her head hopelessly. He put his hand on her arm. She quivered.

'I bought Selby, Laura.'

She stared at him in utter amazement. She couldn't trust herself to speak.

'I did, and it was a lot of money.'

'But you were sitting at the back.'

'Someone was bidding for me. I wanted this house.'

If she hadn't been so shocked, she would have flown at him then for putting them through all that.

'But why did you say you'd pulled out? What were you thinking of?'

'I wasn't thinking. I was mad. But, then, India came to see me.'

'She what?'

'Your aunt put me straight,' he said ever so softly.

'About what?'

'She explained a few things to me, and I to her.'

'Like?

'That I should reconsider my decision. I don't know how to say this,' he added. 'It's quite out of character. I find it difficult. What I'm trying to say is I think the world of you. Ever since that day I saw you in the woods, I really liked you. You were so bad-tempered. You had the same look in your eyes as you do now. I've been an utter fool. You've heard of love at first sight, have you?'

She swallowed. Was this a dream? She let him continue.

'When I realised that you and Selby were one and the same, it was an answer to my prayers. I'm not making much sense, am I?'

'Please, go on,' she whispered.

He sat down beside her and took her two hands in his. She was still reeling at the thought he'd bought Selby and that he was saying all these things to her. Suddenly, it was making sense.

'What did India say to you?' Laura tried to stop her voice trembling.

'She told me the truth about my father!' was the unexpected reply.

'Pardon?'

'Oh, it's a long story. I made her promise she'd tell you herself. The long and short of it is, my father and your aunt had an understanding. They were in love, but her father wouldn't let her get married to mine.'

'Your father was India's secret love?'

Now it was making more sense.

'He wanted her to elope, but out of some sense of—I think she used the word, duty, to her family—she refused and he went off in a huff. You can gather I'm something of a chip off the old block, stubborn and Irish. But he never got over India. He used to talk about this place incessantly. Of course, he never told us why. It would have been too upsetting for my mother. I think he was probably in love with India all his life. He spent a lot of time away, building up the business. And, naturally, when I found out that Selby was on the market, I was interested. And, when I saw you, I was more than that. I was besotted. Like father, like son, I suppose.'

'But why didn't you say?'

'It wouldn't have been the thing, would it? And there was Fiona.'

Laura suddenly felt cold and shivered. Jack reached for the counterpane, pulled it up and around Laura's shoulders.

'I'm not in love with Fiona. I never have been. She had the wrong idea about me all along. She can also be very spiteful.'

'I can believe that.'

133

'We had a massive row after she told me that Nick Quinton and you had something going. He'd told her himself, that he and you were getting married. That way Selby was staying in the family. She packed her bags and went. I didn't want to stand in the way of your happiness, so I pulled out.'

'Jack, it was a complete fabrication on his part. I can't stand him. I know what it looked like when you saw us together. I was actually trying to get away from him. He did ask me to marry him, twice, but I don't even like Nick. It was terrible when you pulled out. I thought he was going to get Selby.'

'I realise that now. India made it clear that you didn't care about him.'

At that moment, Laura didn't know if she ought to strangle her aunt, or kiss her! Pure relief began to wash over her. Selby was safe! Jack O'Neill was free and saying wonderful things. She looked at Jack, sitting there beside her, his eyes saying all the unspoken things she wanted to hear.

'I expect you're very like your father,' she said, putting up her hand and stroking his face.

It all made sense now. India saw his father in him, realised immediately that history was repeating itself in Jack's interest in Laura, perhaps saw him as the son she never had and made sure that the same thing didn't happen all over again. It was like a fairy story.

'I can see you're working it all out,' he said

softly. 'So you're glad I bought Selby?'

'Yes, and I'm more than glad you ditched Fiona,' she replied boldly.

'Come here!' he said huskily and took her in his arms.

It was like coming home. As they lay entwined on the bed and she was gasping for breath after his passionate kisses, he said mischievously, 'By the way, I'm giving you that picture of India for a wedding present. You didn't think you'd outbid me, did you?'

'Is that a proposal?' she asked.

'You know it is,' he said, stretching out his foot.

The next moment, they were jumping up, laughing, as the old harp clattered off its stand on to the floor, emitting an indignant rattle.

We hope you have enjoyed this Large Print book. Other Chivers Press or Thorndike Press Large Print books are available at your library or directly from the publishers.

For more information about current and forthcoming titles, please call or write, without obligation, to:

Chivers Large Print
published by BBC Audiobooks Ltd
St James House, The Square
Lower Bristol Road
Bath BA2 3BH
UK
email: bbcaudiobooks@bbc.co.uk
www.bbcaudiobooks.co.uk

OR

Thorndike Press
295 Kennedy Memorial Drive
Waterville
Maine 04901
USA
www.gale.com/thorndike
www.gale.com/wheeler

All our Large Print titles are designed for easy reading, and all our books are made to last.